The Shadow Pa

A Mystery Story for B

CW01081804

Roy J. Snell

Alpha Editions

This edition published in 2023

ISBN : 9789357972802

Design and Setting By
Alpha Editions
www.alphaedis.com
Email - info@alphaedis.com

As per information held with us this book is in Public Domain.
This book is a reproduction of an important historical work. Alpha Editions uses the
best technology to reproduce historical work in the same manner it was first
published to preserve its original nature. Any marks or number seen are left
intentionally to preserve its true form.

CONTENTS

CHAPTER I
THE SILVER FOX

"And then I saw it—the Shadow."

The speaker's eyes appeared to snap. Johnny Thompson leaned forward in his chair. "It glided through the fog without a sound." The voice droned on, "Not a sound, mind you! We had a small boat with powerful motors. I stepped on the gas. Our motors roared. We were after that shadow."

"And then?" Johnny Thompson whispered.

"For all I know," the black-eyed man murmured, leaning back in his chair, "we might have cut that shadow square in two. Anyway, that's the last we saw of it for that day.

"But think of it!" he exclaimed after a second's pause. "Think of the thing just disappearing in the fog like that!"

He was a romantic figure, this man Blackie. The boys of Matanuska Valley in Alaska loved this gathering of an evening about the red-hot stove in the store. And no part of the evening's entertainment was ever half so thrilling as Blackie's stories.

"It was spring then," Blackie added, "late May, when the salmon run was on."

"It was a whale after salmon, that shadow," someone suggested.

"No, sir!" Blackie fairly shouted. "It was too fast for a whale! Some sort of Oriental craft, I shouldn't wonder. Though how they'd make it go without a sound is beyond me.

"Ah well," he sighed, "I'll be rid of these by spring." He kicked at the crutches beside his chair. "Then I'll be after 'em again, those bloomin' Orientals and their gliding shadows."

"You going back into the Coast Guard Service?" Johnny asked eagerly.

"I sure am!" Blackie agreed heartily. "Boy! That's the life! A speedy boat with two or three airplane motors in her hull, a good crew, plenty of gas, the wide open sea and enough trouble to keep your eyes open day and night. Man! Oh, man!"

"Take me along," Johnny suggested impulsively.

"Me too!" put in Lawrence, his slim, bright-eyed cousin.

"What do you know about boats?" Blackie asked.

"Plenty," was Johnny's prompt reply. "Been on 'em all my life, power boats on the Great Lakes, Carib Indian sailboats in the Caribbean, skin-boats way up north. It's all the same.

"And Lawrence here," he added after a brief pause, "he knows about motors."

"I—I was assistant mechanic in an airplane hangar for a season," Lawrence agreed modestly.

"Well, it—might—be—arranged," Blackie replied slowly. "Don't know about pay. You sort of have to be on regular for that. But up here in the north, things can't always be done according to department regulations. Anyway, it's worth thinking about."

"Thank—oh, thank you," Lawrence stammered. Johnny knew how he was feeling at that moment. He, Johnny, had met adventure in many climes. Lawrence had lived a quiet life. Really to sail on a coast guard boat in search of Orientals suspected of stealing salmon, smuggling or spying off the Alaskan shores, to chase gray shadows that pass in the fog! Worth thinking of? Well, you'd just know it was!

Johnny was still thinking of all this when two hours later, he crept beneath the blankets in the small log cabin room occupied by Lawrence and himself.

"That would be great!" he was telling himself. In fancy, he allowed his mind to wander. Bristol Bay, a hundred and fifty miles wide and a hundred and fifty long, fishing boats on the water, canneries on the shore and back behind all this in the fog somewhere, beyond the three-mile line, great dark bulks that were Oriental ships. Why these ships? No one knew exactly. "Spying out our shore-line," some said, "stealing our salmon," said others. And perhaps they were smugglers. It was known that these ships carried smaller crafts that could be lowered to the water. "Could do anything, go anywhere, these small boats," Johnny assured himself.

"And the Shadow, that mysterious gray form that goes streaking through the fog. What could it be?

"Ah, well," he settled deeper among the blankets. "It's a long time till spring, and here, right in Matanuska Valley is exciting adventure aplenty."

As if reading his thoughts, Lawrence murmured dreamily, "We'll go after him again tomorrow."

"Yes," Johnny agreed, "tomorrow."

"Lawrence! Look! There he is!" Johnny pointed excitedly up the glistening expanse of frozen river. Tomorrow had come. They were on the river.

"Wh—where?" Lawrence whispered.

"You don't have to whisper." Johnny laughed low. "He's way up there. I can scarcely see him with the glass. Here! Take it. See that pool of water on the right side?"

"Yes—yes, I see." Lawrence took the field glasses.

"At this end of that pool. I saw him move. Look quick!"

For a space of ten seconds Lawrence studied that pool. "Yes," he exclaimed at last, "he *is* there! I saw him move over to the right."

"Lawrence!" Johnny's voice was tense with emotion. "I'm going after him!"

Johnny bent over to tighten a skate strap. "Here! Give me the bag. You follow me, but not too fast. You can keep the glasses. I won't need them."

"Al—all right, Johnny. Be careful! You—"

But Johnny was away. Skating from the hips, scarcely lifting a foot from the ice, he appeared to glide without effort over the glass-like surface of the river.

The boy's spirits rose. They were "after him again." And "he" was a grand prize indeed.

"If only we can get him," Johnny was thinking. "If we only can."

The distant future quite forgotten, Johnny was living intensely in the glorious present. Lawrence followed slowly. He, too, was a skillful skater. The river at this point was frozen solidly. No need for thought here. At once his mind was busy with memories of the not-too-distant past and plans for the future.

Life for him had been strange. Eight months before he had been on the broad, dry prairies of the Dakotas. Now he was skating on the Matanuska River in Alaska. Nor was this just an adventurous winter trip. The Matanuska Valley was his home and would be, he hoped, for years to come. Six miles back and up a half mile from the river was their claim and the sod-covered log cabin they called home.

"We are pioneers!" he whispered to himself. "Pioneers!" he repeated softly. How he loved that word. How much it meant to them all; freedom, new life, fresh hope and in the end a home all their own. "And paid for," he declared sturdily.

Yes, when the government had announced a resettlement project in this rich valley and the Lawsons who had been driven from their farm home by drouth and dust heard of it they had joined up. And here they were: father, mother and son, with cousin Johnny thrown in for good measure.

"Been here six months," Lawrence thought. "Got a little start. And next year!" Ah, yes, next year. His face sobered. So much depended on the future. And they needed so many things.

"We'll not go in debt," his father had insisted stoutly. "Not for a single thing we can do without."

But now the boy's mind came back with a snap to the immediate present. As he looked ahead he saw nothing of Johnny. For a second his heart fluttered. Had his good pal come upon an unsuspected air-hole? Had he gone through? Was he, at this moment, caught by the swift current, shooting along rapidly beneath the ice?

"You have to know your river," an old-timer had said to them. "Every foot of it." Did Johnny know it well enough, or—

Of a sudden he let out a low, happy laugh. Some distance ahead, showing among the branches of a fallen fir tree, he had caught a glimpse of Johnny's plaid mackinaw.

"He—he's all right," he breathed. "Just getting a look."

Johnny was now within a hundred yards of that dark pool, where, he hoped, their prize still lurked.

"He must see him with the naked eye," Lawrence murmured as he glided into the shadow of a shelving bank. Here, steadying himself with one hand, he held the glass to his eyes with the other.

Then, with hand trembling so it seemed the glass would drop, he exclaimed, "Man! Oh, man! It's a silver fox and a beauty! If only he gets him! If he does!"

They were hunters, these boys. "Strange hunters!" some might say. "No guns! No traps!" This valley was alive with rich, fur-bearing animals. With guns and traps one might reap a winter's harvest. Without guns or traps how was it to be done! This had been the question uppermost in their minds some weeks before. In the end they had found the answer, or thought they had. And a strange answer it was.

They had arrived, this little family of four homesteaders, along with hundreds of others in the Matanuska Valley, too late in the spring to clear land and raise a crop. They had been obliged to content themselves with a large garden and an acre of potatoes.

Such potatoes as those had been! "We'll sell two hundred bushels!" Lawrence had exulted. "That will go a long way toward buying a small tractor. Then just watch our smoke!"

"Oh, no you won't!" Jack Morgan, an old-time settler in the valley, had laughed.

"What? Why not?" the boy demanded.

"Who'll you sell 'em to?" the old-timer asked in a kindly voice.

"Why, we—we'll ship 'em out."

"You can't, son," Jack's voice rumbled. "That's the trouble. At present there's no market for farm products here. Never has been. That'll be worked out in time, now the government is interested. But just now we have to eat our own potatoes."

"But how do you get any money?" Lawrence had demanded.

"Trap foxes, minks, martin. Good money in trappin'," was the old-timer's reply.

Of course, the boys had come rushing home bursting with the news that they could make money all winter long trapping.

To their surprise they saw Lawrence's father's smiling face draw into sober lines.

"No, boys," he said quietly. "Not that. Anything but trapping. It's too cruel. I'd rather you went out with a gun."

"But we haven't a gun," Lawrence protested.

"That's right," the father agreed. "And it's not to be regretted.

"You see, boys," his face took on a strange look, "when I was about ten years old I had a dog I thought the world and all of. He didn't cost a lot of money. Never won any prizes at dog shows. But his hair was kinky, his eyes alive with fun and his bark a joyous sound to hear. No boy ever had a more faithful friend than good old Bing.

"And then," his voice grew husky, "well, you see there was a man who lived all by himself down by the river, Skunk McGee they called him. Never amounted to much, he didn't. But he trapped enough skunks and muskrats to pay for his groceries.

"Our farm was along the river, on both sides. Father told him more than once not to set his traps on our farm.

"One time in the dead of winter, way down below zero, old Bing didn't come home. I was worried but father said, 'He's gone to the neighbors and they took him in on account of its being so cold.'

"But he hadn't," Mr. Lawson's tone changed abruptly. "He was in one of Skunk McGee's traps. And when we found him he was dead, frozen hard as a rock.

"And so you see, boys," he added quietly, "I've always hated traps. I never see one even now but I seem to see poor old Bing with one foot in it, whining and shivering out there all alone."

From that day on the thought of traps was banished from their minds.

But the foxes? Did they vanish? No indeed! The foxes saw to it that they were not forgotten.

Before the summer was at an end some families, unaccustomed to the pioneer life, lost courage and decided to return to their original homes. Among these were two families who had brought with them small flocks of chickens. By careful planning the Lawsons were able to buy the chickens. Having built a stout log henhouse and a small wire enclosure for sunny days, they felt better than ever prepared for the winter.

"Chicken for Thanksgiving and Christmas and eggs all winter long! What luck!" Lawrence rejoiced.

The chickens, no doubt, were something of a surprise to the foxes. But had they not always preyed upon ptarmigan? And were not chickens just big plump ptarmigan? Perhaps this was the way they reasoned. At any rate, one night Lawrence heard a loud squawking and rushed out just in time to see a plump white hen vanish into the night. A fox had her by the neck.

"Something must be done about that," he insisted at once. "If we can't trap the foxes, what then?"

"Take them alive," was his father's prompt reply.

"Alive! Alive!" both boys cried.

"I can't see why not," was Lawrence's father's quiet reply. "Of course, you'll have to wear tough, moose-hide mittens and keep your noses out of reach, but—"

"We'll do it," Lawrence exclaimed. "But then," his face sobered, "how'll we ever catch up with a fox?"

"When I was a boy," said his father, "we used to catch muskrats on skates."

"Muskrats on skates?" Lawrence laughed.

"We were on the skates," his father corrected with a smile. "The rats were on the ice, you see," he leaned forward. "We worked it this way. We'd watch until the muskrat came out of his hole to get a drink. He'd go to an open pool of water at the edge of the ice. We'd wait until he'd started back across the ice. Then we'd come swooping down on him. He'd get frightened and sprawl all over the ice—no wild creature can handle himself well on the ice. So we had him.

"Once," he chuckled, "Bob Barnett saw something moving on the ice. It was just getting dark. He thought it was a rat. He come swooping down upon it and—" he paused to chuckle. "Well, it turned out to be a skunk. The skunk objected to his intrusion. So Bob went home to bury his clothes—just for a scent."

The boys joined in the laugh that followed but they were not slow in following this suggestion. They found, however, that great skill and caution were needed in this type of hunting.

They made progress slowly. After catching two muskrats, a snow-shoe rabbit and two ground-squirrels, they decided to start a small zoo all their own.

"Who knows?" Lawrence enthused. "We may catch some truly rare creature. The keepers of zoos are always on the lookout for live specimens. We may sell enough to get that bright new tractor down at Palmer after all."

"A tractor!" Johnny doubted. "Oh! No! Surely not that much!"

"And yet," Lawrence now thought as he stood watching for Johnny's next move on the river ice, "there he is creeping up on a silver fox. What is a real, live silver fox worth?" To this exciting question he could form no accurate answer. He had a hazy recollection of reading somewhere about one that was sold for $3000.00.

"No such luck as that," he whispered.

Just now, however, his attention was directed toward the silver fox that, still very much at liberty, had taken a good drink from the pool and was standing, nose in air, apparently looking, listening, smelling. Had he smelled trouble? Would he drop into the pool to swim across and disappear on the farther bank, or would he start back across that glistening stretch of ice? Lawrence felt his heart leap as he saw the fox drop his head. The big moment was at hand.

"He—he's going across!" he exclaimed in a hoarse whisper. "It means so much!" His thoughts went into a tailspin. Not only would they possess a real, live silver fox for which, beyond doubt, some zoo would pay handsomely, but their flock of chickens would be safe, for they could tell by the size of the tracks that he was the one that was getting the chickens. He was a sly one, indeed, this fox. Three times in the last month, in spite of their every effort to prevent it, he had carried off a fat old hen.

"He—Johnny's starting," Lawrence said, as, gliding silently from cover, he prepared to follow his cousin on his swift, silent, breathless quest.

It was a truly wonderful sight, those two boys moving as if pushed by an unseen hand closer, ever closer to the unsuspecting fox.

Moving swiftly, Johnny reached a fallen cottonwood tree. Just then the fox, pausing in his course, once more sniffed the air. "I might get him if I rushed him now," he thought, "and I might miss." This was true. The fox was but a third of the way across the ice. He was still too close to the pool. The plan was to allow him to reach the very center of the river, then to rush him. Startled, he would start quickly for some shore. Losing all sense of caution, he would begin to sprawl upon the ice. As the boy came rushing on with the speed of the wind, he would stoop over, snatch at the fox and speed on. He must seize the fox just back of his ears. Could he do it? As he stood there hidden his pulse pounded madly. He, too, had seen that it was a silver fox.

"He—he's smelled me!" The boy's voice rose in a sudden shrill shout. "Come on, Lawrence! I'm going after him! Bring the bag!"

Gripping a large, moose-hide sack, Lawrence went speeding after him.

As for Johnny, with breath-taking suddenness, he saw the distance between him and the fox fade. A hundred yards, fifty, twenty, and—"Now!" he breathed. "Now!"

The fox was not a foot from the edge of the pool when, still speeding wildly, the boy bent down and made one wild grab.

"Got him!" he shouted exultantly. But wait! Ten seconds more and the fox's ivory teeth were flashing in his very face. He seemed to feel them tearing at his nose. There was nothing to do but drop him. With a suddenness, startling even to the fox, the boy let go.

Down dropped the fox. On sped the boy. When Lawrence reached the spot the fox had vanished into a hole and Johnny was skating slowly, mournfully back.

"Never mind," Lawrence consoled. "We'll get him another time."

"But a silver fox and a beauty!" Johnny exclaimed. "Think of losing him!"

"I have thought." Lawrence was able to grin in spite of his disappointment. "It would have meant a lot and now—" he chuckled, "now we know it's a real silver fox after our chickens. We'll have to lock them in a vault."

"Not as bad as that," said Johnny. "But Lawrence," his voice dropped. "This must remain a deep secret. Not a word to anyone. If Jim and Jack Mayhorn knew about this there'd be a trap on every foot of the river."

"Never a word," Lawrence agreed.

They were a rather disconsolate pair as they pulled off their skates a half hour later.

"To think!" Johnny groaned. "I had my hands on five hundred dollars, perhaps a thousand dollars worth of fox and had to drop it because it was too hot."

"The price of a tractor," Lawrence agreed. "It's too bad."

It was too bad indeed. All day, five days in the week, they worked hard at clearing land. The trees were coming down. After the spring thaw thousands of stumps must be pulled. A tractor would do that work. After that it would draw the plows.

"If only I hadn't lost him!" Johnny groaned.

"Aw! Forget it!" Lawrence exclaimed. "Come on! Let's go home by the camp."

The "camp," as they had come to call it, was a three-sided shelter built on a corner of their forty-acre claim. It had been built, and apparently abandoned, only a few months before their arrival. Such a snug shelter was it that the boys had often sought its protection from storms. Once, with a roaring fire before its open side, they had spent a night sleeping on its bed of evergreen boughs.

The place never lost its fascination. Who had built it? Trader, hunter, trapper or gold prospector? To this question they could form no answer. Would he some day return? To this, strangely enough on this very afternoon they were to discover the answer, at least that which appeared to be the answer. As they were looking it over for the twentieth time Lawrence suddenly exclaimed, "Look! Here's a bit of cloth tacked to this post. And there's a note written on it in indelible ink!"

Johnny did look. "Read it!" he exclaimed.

"I will," Lawrence began to read. "Can't quite make it out," he murmured. "Oh, yes, this is it.

"'I WILL BE BACK ON JULY 1st. BILL.'"

"So he's coming back," Johnny's tone was strange.

"Coming back," Lawrence agreed. "All right, Bill, old boy," he laughed. "We'll keep your snug little camp ship-shape till you arrive."

And for this bit of service, had they but known it, they were to receive a very unusual reward.

CHAPTER II
BLACKIE'S STORY

"Tell us how you got that game leg of yours, Blackie," Joe Lawrence, the Palmer store-keeper, said to Blackie, as they all sat about the roaring steel-barrel stove three nights later.

"Oh, that—" Blackie did not reply at once.

Johnny and Lawrence were by the fire. They had walked in from the claim, a frosty three miles, with the thermometer at twenty-five degrees below. They were not the sort of boys who loaf about stores and pool halls, listening to cheap talk. Far from that. They had come to make a purchase or two and, in an hour, with the steel-blue stars above them would be on their way home. Just now the fire felt good.

"Sure, tell us," Johnny encouraged.

"Hello! You here?" Blackie demanded, as if he had not seen them before. "What'd you come in for on a night like this?"

"Wedges," said Johnny. "Steel wedges for splitting logs."

"Wedges." There came a hoarse laugh from the corner. It was Jack Mayhorn who spoke. "Who wants wedges in this country? Do like I do. Cut down the trees that split easy."

"They've all got tough spots," Johnny replied quietly. "Where the limbs have been cut off."

"Oh, the knotty pines!" Jack laughed again. "Roll 'em into the fence row an' leave 'em. That's the way we do."

"We don't," said Lawrence. "We aim to take them as they come, tough or not tough, they've got to bust."

"Why?" Blackie fixed his piercing black eyes on the boy.

"I—I don't know why," was Lawrence's slow reply. "I can't explain it right." The boy hesitated. "But I—you know—I sort of hate being licked, even by a tough log. So I—we sort of take 'em as they come."

"That's great!" Blackie slapped his knee. "And I suppose you feel the same way?" he asked of Johnny.

"Sure do," was Johnny's prompt reply. "They can't come too tough for me."

"Can't come too tough for little old Johnny." There was a sneer in Jack Mayhorn's voice. "But he's afraid to set traps or carry a rifle."

"Not afraid," Johnny replied quietly. "Just don't want to."

"Tell us, Blackie," Joe, the store-keeper, broke in, sensing a possible row, "tell us how you got that leg."

Even then Blackie did not comply at once. Turning to the boys, he said in a low tone, "You boys are dead right. No use letting a log or anything else lick you." Dropping his voice still lower he added, "I might take you with me next spring on that coast guard boat. I just might, that is, if you still want to go."

Then in a changed voice he said, "All right, Joe, I'll tell you all about that leg of mine, though I'm not fond of doing it. It always makes me hopping mad, just thinking about it.

"You see," he went on at once, "I was up a river in Asia. Doesn't matter which river. I was in the navy. Less than six months ago, although it seems two years. I was on a small U. S. gunboat. What one? That doesn't matter, either. She's at the bottom of the river now." He paused to stare at the fire.

"We were laying up the river. There was fighting down below. We'd come up-river to get out of the way. The fighting was foolish enough, but none of our business.

"We were there to protect American citizens. There were twenty or more of them on board, reporters and missionaries and the like.

"I'd just come on duty when a big bombing plane came hovering, like a vulture, over us. It circled off again. 'Good riddance,' I said to my buddy.

"I hadn't finished saying it when it came zooming back. This time higher up and—" Blackie took a long breath. "The bloomin' infidels! What do you think? They let go a bomb that missed us by inches.

"You should have seen us scatter," Blackie laughed in spite of himself.

And then, of a sudden, the lines between his eyes grew deep and long. "They bombed us. They sank our ship. My buddy was killed. I caught it in the leg. I got a lifeboat off, doing what I could to save the women.

"Me," he faltered. "I'm no sort of a story teller. But I hope I'm something of a fighter. This old leg will be good as new next spring. And, sure's I'm living, I'm going hunting little brown men up there in Bristol Bay. They stole a cool million dollars' worth of fish last season. How many'll they get this year? That depends on the Coast Guard men and, glory be! I'm one of them. I'm out of the navy, invalided home, back on the good old job, and there'll be plenty of things a-popping in May.

"Er, excuse me, boys," he apologized. "That sounds an awful lot like bragging. We didn't catch the Shadow that passes in the fog last season. We didn't do those Orientals much harm, either. Too slick for us, I guess. But wish me luck next time. The biggest industry in Alaska, the run of red salmon, depends on us."

"Here's luck," said Johnny, lifting a cup of coffee just poured by Joe's motherly wife. "Here's luck to the service."

"And may you be my buddy!" Blackie added.

That night Johnny and Lawrence walked home in silence. The great white world was all about them and the blue-white stars above. Their thoughts were long, long thoughts.

Arrived at their log cabin home, they dragged out a tattered map of Alaska to study its shore-line and most of all the shores of Bristol Bay.

"May," Lawrence said at last. "That's a long time yet."

"Yes," Johnny agreed, "and there's plenty to get excited about tomorrow. What do you say we turn in?"

CHAPTER III
FAT AND FURIOUS

Anyone who had watched the two boys skating slowly up the river next morning would surely have been puzzled. Before them, now darting up a steep bank and now scurrying along over the snow, were two brown, fur-clad creatures. Neither dogs nor cats, they still appeared quite domestic in their actions. Once when they had gone racing ahead too far Johnny let out a shrill whistle and they came dashing back to peer up into his face as if to say, "Did you call me?"

"They're great!" Lawrence chuckled. "Got a dog beat a mile. They never bark."

"And yet they can find where wild creatures live," Johnny agreed.

Just now, as you no doubt have guessed, the boys were looking for the spot, under some great rock or at the foot of a tree, which the silver fox called his home.

"We must find him," Johnny had exclaimed only an hour before.

"We surely must," Lawrence had agreed.

And indeed they must, for three principal reasons. Last night the fox had, by shrewd cunning, managed to pry the chicken coop door open and made off with a rooster. The fox was worth a lot of money—they were sure of this—dead or alive. They must get him before someone with a gun or with traps got sight of him. And they must take him alive, if possible—a very large contract.

Their desires had been redoubled by something that had happened only the night before. Mack Gleason, the settler whose claim joined them on the west, had been in for a friendly chat.

"Got your tractor yet?" he had asked of Mr. Lawson.

"Not yet," had been the reply.

"Well, you better hurry. They're going fast. May not be another shipment until it is too late for spring's work."

"No money just now."

"Money!" Mack exploded. "Who said anything about money? Government gives 'em to you on time."

"But time has a way of rolling around," Mr. Lawson had replied quietly.

"Oh, the Government wouldn't be hard on you," Mack laughed. "Look at us. We've got a washing machine and a buzz-saw, and a motor to run 'em, a tractor, plow, harrow, everything, and all on time."

"Yes, I know," had come in the same slow, quiet tones. "And I know the Government won't be hard on you. Still it will want its money, same as any loaning agency. It just has to be that way.

"This week," Mr. Lawson went on after a moment, "I received a letter from an old friend of mine. Few years back he secured a government loan on his home. He didn't keep up the interest and payments. They took it from him. Now he's unhappy about it. But people who borrow must pay. That's why we're trying not to borrow."

"And we won't, not if we can help it." Lawrence set his will hard as he now followed those dark brown creatures over the ice.

"Johnny," he said suddenly. "Do you think father should let us use traps?"

"I—I don't know," Johnny replied slowly. "But that, for us, is not the question. Ours is, 'Have we a right to urge him to let us use them?'

"And the answer is, 'No,'" he chuckled. "So we'll have to trust our little old otters to lead the way. When they find Mr. Silver Fox for us we'll have to grab him."

"If only one of those trapping fellows doesn't get him first," Lawrence said, wrinkling his brow.

Early in the season, as, with dreamy eyes, the boys wandered over the forty acres of land that was, they hoped, to be their home for years to come, they had caught the low, whining notes of some small creatures apparently in distress.

"It comes from under that rock," Johnny had said.

"No, over here beneath this dead tree trunk," Lawrence insisted.

He was right. Having torn away the decayed stump, they had found two round, brown balls of fur. These balls were baby otters. Taking them home, they had raised them on a bottle. And now, here they were, paying their debt by scouting about in search of the silver fox.

Pets they were, the grandest in all the world. The happiest moments of their young lives were these long hikes. Never once did it seem to occur to them that it might be nice to desert their young masters and answer the call of the wild.

Now, as the boys followed them, they went gliding here and there peeking into every crack and crevice of ice or frozen shore. From time to time they poked their noses into some hole into which strange tracks had vanished. After a good sniff they put their heads together and uttered low whining noises. These noises varied with their opinions on the condition of each particular hole. At times they appeared to shake their heads and whine, "Too bad. He was here three hours ago. Now he's gone."

At other times they put their noses in the air and sang triumphantly, "He's there. He's right in that hole this minute."

Had the boys been able to train their pets to go in the hole and frighten out the prey, they might have held a moose-hide sack at the entrance to each hole and added quite rapidly to their collection of living Arctic animals. This, however, the otters would not do. They were not looking for a fight. And indeed, why should they? They did not live upon squirrels and muskrats, but upon fish. "We'll find 'em, you catch 'em," seemed to be their motto.

For the boys, finding the lair of the silver fox would not insure his capture. It merely meant that they would know where he lived and would watch that spot in the hope that he might come out on the ice in search of food or a drink and that then they might come speeding in to grab him.

"Look!" Lawrence exclaimed suddenly, "there are Old Silver's tracks!"

"Yes, sir! He just cut in from the hill to the river. He—" Suddenly Johnny broke off to peer upstream.

"Something moving up there," he whispered. "Maybe—"

But the otters had smelled the fox tracks and were off on swift tracking feet. Johnny bent over to examine those tracks.

"It's the old fellow or his brother," he murmured. "No other fox around here has such large feet. Boy! He's a humdinger!"

Once more his keen eyes swept the upper reaches of the river. "Huh!" he grunted. "Whatever that was, it's vanished now."

"Might as well follow the otters," Lawrence suggested.

They did follow. Soft-footed in silence they tracked on for a mile. Up banks and down again, over a ridge, back to the river. "Look at those feathers!" Lawrence whispered.

"Got a ptarmigan," said Johnny. "After that he should have made a bee line for his lair."

That was just what the fox had done. Straight as an arrow he had returned to the stream, then he had sped away along its course until he came to a huge gray rock. There the trail ended. And beneath this rock, according to the verdict of the two singing otters, he must still lie fast asleep.

"Good old otters!" Lawrence exclaimed in a hoarse whisper.

"They've found us his hiding place," Johnny agreed. "And will we watch it? We—"

Suddenly he broke off short to point excitedly upstream.

"A bear cub!" Lawrence exclaimed low. "He's going to cross the river."

"We—we'll get on our sk-ates," said Johnny excitedly. "Then let's take him."

"Can we?" Lawrence was doubtful.

"Sure! We'll lasso him and tie him up. He'll make a grand addition to our zoo. Come on!"

Swinging out on the shining ice, skating silently from the hips, the boys glided like two dark ghosts toward the unsuspecting bear cub who, at that moment, had started to cross a broad stretch of slippery ice. Sly silence is, however, a game that two can play at. This the boys were to learn very soon and to their sorrow.

One day the boys had come, quite unexpectedly, upon a half-grown white caribou, or perhaps it had been a reindeer, that had wandered down from some far northern herd. However that might have been, they were filled with regret at the thought that they were not equipped for capturing it for their "zoo." From that time on they had carried lariats and, by way of some added safety, short, stout spears. They were thus equipped today as they sped swiftly, silently toward the bear cub.

"I'll toss the lasso over his head, then you watch the fun," Johnny chuckled.

"I'll watch all right," Lawrence agreed. And he did.

Slowly, clumsily, the young bear, no larger than a good-sized dog, made his way across the ice. The wind was away from him. He could not smell the intruders, nor was he aware of their presence until, with a sudden rush, Johnny was upon him.

Never will the boy forget the look of surprise that came over the young bear's comical face as he stared straight into his eyes. The whole affair was easy, too easy. He passed so close to the cub that he might have touched him. He did not. Instead, he dropped his noose over his head, pulled it tight, then, letting out slack, whirled about to face the cub. What would the cub do about that? He was to know instantly. Throwing himself back on his haunches, the cub began backing and pulling like a balky horse. On his skates, Johnny was no match for him. All he could do was to come along. To his further annoyance, he found that his lariat had whirled about his wrist and tied itself into a knot. As long as the cub kept the line tight he could not untie the knot. He did not quite relish the idea of dashing up to the cub and saying, "By your leave, I'll untie this knot." So, for the moment, he played into the cub's hand.

Then the unexpected happened. With a grunt and a snarl of rage, a huge black bear, the cub's mother beyond a possible doubt, dashed over a ridge to come charging straight at Johnny and the cub.

"Hey! Hey! Look out!" Lawrence shouted. "Drop your rope and beat it."

"I—I can't," Johnny cried in sudden consternation. "He—he's got me tied."

"Tied!" Lawrence gasped.

"It's 'round my wrist." Johnny watched wide-eyed while the huge mother bear came tobogganing down the high, steep river bank. She hit the ice like a bobsled and, dropping on hind legs and tail, came sliding straight on.

Just in time, Johnny came to his senses and began doing a back-stroke. Only by inches did he miss the husky swing of the angry bear's paw.

"Cut the rope," Lawrence shouted.

"Al-all right, I'll—I'll cut it." Johnny dug into a pocket with his free hand. A pocket knife. It must be opened. With one eye on the cub, who for the moment sat whining, and the other upon the mother bear, who was scrambling awkwardly to her feet, he had no eyes left for his knife. Just as, having gripped the handle with one hand, the blade with the other, he managed to open the knife, the cub, going into frenzied action, gave him a sudden jerk that sent the knife spinning far out on the ice.

"It's gone," he groaned.

No more time for this. Old mother bear was after him. Fortunately this old bear was heavy with fat. She had been preparing for a winter's sleep. Still she could travel and she was fat and furious. Her skill as a skater was something to marvel at.

Since he could not escape from the rope, the only thing for Johnny to do was circle. Circle he did. One time around with the bear at his heels; two times around he had gained a little; three times around he caught the gleam of his knife. Could he stoop and pick it up? He bent over, made a reach for it, struck a crack with his skate and all but fell.

"I—I'll get it next time," he breathed.

To his surprise he found that next time the knife was well out of his reach. Then to his utter horror, he saw that the perverse cub was standing still, making an animated Maypole out of himself and that it would be no time at all until the rope would be all wound around him. They would meet face to face, cub, mother bear and boy. And after that? He shuddered as he sped along that ever-narrowing circle.

"I'm coming in," Lawrence shouted.

"No, you—"

Johnny could say no more. Lawrence was already in. Skating straight at the bear to attract her attention, Lawrence shot past her and slapped her sharply on the nose.

It was a daring and effective endeavor. Turning with a snarl, completely abandoning her cub at this fancied insult, the bear went after him with a rush.

That was all right as far as it went. The skating was good. The bear was fast, but not fast enough to catch him. There is, however, an end to all things. There was an end to that stretch of ice. It ended in a series of rapids that were not frozen over.

Lawrence groaned as he saw open water ahead. To his added terror, he saw that the river narrowed at that point. That the bear could outrun him on land he knew all too well.

"Got to be an artful dodger," he told himself.

At that moment how he rejoiced that he had trained himself as a hockey skater. Swinging about in a half circle, he sped toward the right-hand bank. But the bear was there ahead of him.

Just as she reared up for a sledge-hammer blow, the boy whirled squarely about and shot away to left. Again he was too late for a safe passage, but not so much too late. He was gaining. Three more times, then with a joyous intake of breath he shot past the bear and was away.

In the meantime, Johnny, safe for the moment from the mother bear, had hastily unwound the surprised cub, then had rushed him with such speed that the rope was off his neck before he could lift a paw. The cub was free. So was Johnny. And there were no regrets.

"Johnny," said Lawrence as he joined his companion five minutes later, "I don't think we want any bears in our zoo. They're too playful." They were to change their minds about this, but that was to come sometime later.

"That," said Johnny with a chuckle, "was almost funny."

"Yes," Lawrence agreed, "almost." He did not laugh. "Almost, but not quite."

A moment later he exclaimed, "Johnny! Where are the otters? We can't lose them."

"They'll probably hunt us up. They—" Johnny broke off short. "Look!" he murmured low. "Look! There's the silver fox. He's out of his hole. He—he's going to cross the ice."

Lawrence glanced back to the spot where the bears had been. They had vanished. "This time," he whispered, "we'll get that old silver fox. We simply must."

CHAPTER IV
THE CAPTURE OF OLD SILVER

Johnny felt his pulse quicken as he sped along over the ice. The silver fox had come out of the hole. There could be no doubt of that. Would he dodge back in again or would he start across the ice?

"If he starts!" the boy breathed.

He must not be too fast nor too sure. Last time he had muffed a glorious chance. Slowing up, he slid in behind a clump of elders and came to a standstill. There, gripping a shrub, he stood trembling like a butterfly ready for flight.

As for Lawrence, he was coming on more slowly. Naturally more cautious than his cousin, he had an eye out for trouble. That fat old mother bear might still be lurking among the ridges. He had not forgotten how she had come charging down upon them.

"Can't take unnecessary chances," he told himself. "Life is wonderful. I am sure that taking unnecessary chances is wrong. It is making light of God's great gift to us—life."

Ah, yes, it was good to live just now. For the first time in their lives his little family felt sure of having a home of their own. As he glided slowly along he thought of the summer's struggle. At first it had been damp and bitterly cold. Then the sun had been hot and the mosquitoes had come in swarms.

Through all this they had labored on; father, mother, and these two stout boys. It was said that gangs of men would be along to clear patches of land and build cabins. To this they had not listened. "We came to make our own way," they insisted. "We are pioneers. Pioneers must work."

When garden and potato patches were planted they had started the cabin. Selecting, from near and far, trees that were dead but not decayed, they had built a cabin whose walls would not warp and shrink as would those built of green timber.

Later, in the autumn when sharp winds told of a long winter ahead, they had cut squares of tough sod and piled them about the cabin until it seemed a sod house. When the question of a heating stove had arisen, they had discovered an abandoned gasoline barrel, had cut one hole for a door, another for the stove-pipe, had done a little drilling and riveting, and thus had made a stove that, fed on crackling fir logs, laughed at the Arctic cold.

"Pioneers!" he whispered. "We are pioneers." How he loved that thought.

Of a sudden his attention was drawn from past to present by Johnny's beckoning hand. With a quick twisting glide, he moved silently forward until he was at his companion's side.

"Look," Johnny gripped his arm. "There is the fox. He hasn't started across yet and—"

"And there are the otters!" Lawrence broke in with a shrill whisper.

"Yes," Johnny agreed. "That's the queer part of it. They came just so close to the fox, then seemed to shout something at him."

"Like one boy daring another to come out and fight," Lawrence laughed low.

"Yes, or inviting him to a game of tag," whispered Johnny. "And look! There he goes! There goes the fox! Good old otters! They are helping— helping a lot."

He had spoken the truth, the fox was after one of the otters.

"Little good it will do him," Lawrence chuckled. "Those otters are more at home on ice and in water than on land."

"Listen!" Johnny's voice was tense now. His figure stiffened. "In a minute I'm going after him. I've got the bag. If I get him I'll pop him inside. I won't miss now. You just follow along slowly. I might need you."

"Al-all right," the younger boy agreed.

There might have been boys who would have said, "This is my turn. You muffed last time." Not so Lawrence. All too well he knew the skill and natural daring of his cousin. And, after all, in their little family the rule had ever been, "Each for all and all for each." So he watched his cousin glide silently out for one more adventure.

Ten seconds later in watching the little drama of wild life being played there on the ice, he had all but forgotten Johnny. Never before had he seen the tame otters put on such a clever show. Just as the larger one had so far escaped the onrush of the fox that he was becoming discouraged, the small otter, with cunning and extreme daring, slipped up and all but shouted in the fox's ear. At once, the now thoroughly angered fox turned to dash after this second intruder.

No sooner had the first otter been abandoned than he turned about to begin slipping up on the fox to dare him for one more race.

"For all the world like a game of tag!" Lawrence murmured.

All this was aiding Johnny, though it is to be doubted whether the otters knew the value of their antics. The fox was being led farther and farther out on the ice. At the same time his attention was so held by this strange game that he was almost certain to miss catching sight of the boy who now glided closer, ever closer to him.

"Good old otters!" Johnny repeated in a whisper as, drawing his moose-hide mittens tight, he prepared for the final dash.

"He's going after him," Lawrence thought as, with a thrill shooting up his spine, he glided from his sheltered spot, ready, if need be, to come in on the finish.

With a suddenness that must have been startling to the keenest eyes, Johnny swept down upon the fox and the otters. Did the otters see him? Beyond doubt. They saw everything. But the fox? For once he was caught quite unawares. One startled look, a quick squatting down on the ground, and Johnny was at his side. Before the fox could relax from this stiff pose, Johnny's hands, like a brass collar, were about his neck.

"You got him!" Lawrence shouted, springing into action. "You got him! Hurray!"

Then a terrible thing happened. Overjoyed at their great good fortune, Lawrence for the moment lost his bearing. Of a sudden his skate struck ice that crunched ominously. He tripped to go plunging forward into the black waters of the racing river. He had fallen into an open pool.

"I'll drown," he thought, as, in an involuntary manner, he struck out with his hands in a swimming motion. All too late he saw ice ahead. Next instant he was beneath the river's ice.

Johnny saw all this. With a gasp of terror he all but dropped the fox. Then, scarcely knowing what he did, he thrust the fox as if he were his mother's fur scarf, into the moose-hide bag, drew the strings tight, then shot away toward the spot from which his cousin had vanished.

As Lawrence shot beneath the ice, life seemed near its end. Yet there had never been a time when life had seemed so real and so joyous as now. For a second panic gripped him. Holding his breath, he tried to think.

In an instant his mind was clear. He knew what he should do. There were two open pools farther on. How far? He did not know exactly. Could he hold his breath till then? He must hope. And he must try to move over closer to the shelving bank. If he reached the pool he might then touch bottom.

Desperately he struggled to draw himself over to the left. His head hummed. His lungs were bursting, his heart pounding.

"It—it's the end," he thought.

And then, up he popped. Just in time, as his feet touched, he gripped the edge of the ice and held there. Ten agonizing seconds he clung there, then a voice shouted, "Hold on, I'm coming."

Ten seconds more and Johnny, who had leaped to the bank and raced along it, reached out to grip his mackinaw.

"Now!" he shouted. "Out you come." And out he came.

Weak from excitement and exhaustion, he lay there for a time motionless.

"This won't do," Johnny exclaimed at last. "We've got to get going. Here," he dragged the sodden mackinaw from his cousin's shoulders, then put his own sheep-lined coat in its place. After putting his own dry mittens on Lawrence's hands, he pulled him to his feet.

"It's you for skates and the ice, then home as fast as ever you can." He pushed him on before him.

As his skates touched the ice Lawrence felt new warm blood racing through his veins. He was off with the speed of the wind. And after him, with a moose-hide sack dangling at his side and filled with one very angry silver fox, came his loyal, anxious yet joyous friend and cousin, Johnny.

The day, for this part of the world, was not extremely cold. Lawrence's trousers froze into pipe-like forms, but his sturdy, youthful body resisted the cold and sent him speeding on his way.

Dropping down on the river bank at last, they dragged off their skates to take the usual short cut through the timber.

As he passed the carefully built shelter beside that narrow stream, Johnny recalled the note tacked to a post and wondered afresh whether the mysterious Bill would arrive, just as the note said he would, on July 1st.

"Who do you suppose he left that note for?" he exclaimed suddenly.

"Haven't—the—slightest-notion," Lawrence panted, still racing along. "One—thing—is—sure. I'm—going—to—be—there—when that day comes."

"We'll both be there," Johnny agreed. Somehow, as he thought of it, in a strange way it seemed that Bill and the silver fox must in some way be associated with each other. "Pure moonbeams," he assured himself, yet the thought remained in the back of his mind.

There is something in the north that is called "Grapevine telegraph." This name is given to the mysterious means by which, in a land devoid of telephone and telegraph, news travels fast and far. Was it this unreal telegraph that, six hours later, as Lawrence, none the worse for his experience, lay before the roaring fire, brought a stranger to their door? Who can say? Be that as it may, there he was.

"Excuse me for intruding," said the tall, smiling stranger as he brushed the snow from his moccasins. "I heard you'd got a silver fox and I just had to have a look at him. It's been three years since I saw one. I'm Jim Clem. Got a claim over on the other side of the settlement."

"You—you've seen silver foxes." Johnny was on his feet.

"Hundreds of 'em." The stranger smiled.

"Hun-hundreds," Johnny stammered. "I thought they were rare."

"Used to be," admitted Jim Clem. "Still are, fairly so. Did you get a good one?"

"Yes, I—well," Johnny whirled about. "I'll show you." Opening the back door, he dragged in a small wire cage. "We just put him in this for a little while," he half apologized.

"Oh! He's alive. Hurt much?" Jim asked.

"Not hurt at all."

"Not hurt?" Jim stared. "How'd you catch him?"

"With my hands," Johnny chuckled. Then, seeing that this would not stand as a bare statement, he explained briefly their method of capture.

"Say-ee," Jim exclaimed, dropping into a chair, "you're regular natives. And that's a fine specimen. Time was when you'd get two thousand dollars for him."

"Yes, we—"

"But not now," Jim broke in. "Never again. Know much about foxes?"

"No, we—"

"Then, I'll tell you." Jim settled back in his chair. "I worked on a silver fox farm for three years. 'Million Dollar Farm,' they called it. And that's what it was. Raised only silver foxes.

"But you don't get that way all at once," he laughed. "Not by a great deal. Take that fellow you got there. Suppose you find him a mate and decide to start raising silver foxes. Pretty soon you'd have a lovely lot of cute little fox cubs. But would they be silver foxes? Not one. That's almost certain."

"Not one?" Lawrence sat up.

"That's it," Jim agreed. "You'd get two or three little red foxes and, with great luck, a cross fox, that's all."

"You see," he leaned forward, "a silver fox is a freak, just as a half-white robin is. If a half-white robin hatches his eggs his young ones are likely to be jolly little robin redbreasts, nothing more.

"Only by keeping foxes for years and years can you at last hope to raise pure silver foxes. That takes thousands and thousands of dollars. Four brothers went in for that in a big way years ago. Last year they sold 13,000 pelts for more than $1,000,000. And that," he added, "figures up to something like $77.00 apiece."

"That's what our fox is worth," Lawrence groaned. "And we'd have to kill him to get that?"

"Oh, sure," Jim grinned. "But truly," his face sobered, "that's the tough part about fox farming. In the end you've got to kill 'em, so some fine lady can drape their skins about her neck."

"I'd never sell ours to a fox farm," Lawrence said with conviction.

"How about selling him alive to some zoo?" Johnny asked hopefully.

"Don't know very much about that," Jim replied slowly. "I wouldn't hope too much. There are 5,000 fox farms these days. And they raise some beauties.

"But if you mean to keep this fellow alive," he added, "you want to get a wooden barrel and make it into a den for him. Pack it all 'round with chaff and moss to make it warm. Then build him a wire pen all about it. He'll get along fine if you do that.

"I'll have to trot along." He rose to go. "Come and see me. I'll tell you more about 'em. They're interesting no end, foxes are." He bade them goodnight.

"Well," Johnny drawled slowly, "Old Silver won't buy us a tractor, that's sure."

"No," said Lawrence. "But we can learn a lot about him and we can at least keep him from eating our chickens. Don't give up the ship. We'll happen onto something yet."

There are other rewards than money in this life of ours. Remarkable achievement of any sort usually brings us kind words of deserved praise from our fellowmen. It was so with Johnny and Lawrence. More than one settler had suffered from the night raids of Old Silver. Now that he was in prison his captors were highly praised.

Still the problem remained; should they give up their dream of complete independence and go in debt for a tractor?

"I think you'd better," said Johnny. "There are only a few left and they are going fast."

"There'll always be the Titan," Lawrence laughed.

"Yes, the Titan," Johnny agreed. "But who could ever pay for that tractor?"

The Titan was a powerful new type of tractor. Only one had been brought on and that one was priced at a cool thousand dollars.

"We'll wait a little longer," was Mr. Lawson's decision. "The tide of fortune may turn our way."

CHAPTER V
JOHNNY FIGHTS FOR FUN

News travels fast in the north. When the time came for the boys to make one more journey to the store at Palmer everyone had heard of their catch.

"Here they come," someone shouted as, stamping the snow from their feet, they entered the smoke-filled room.

"Here they come. They bring 'em back alive!" someone else shouted.

"Well," Lawrence drawled, "we bring them anyway. Got two minks today. That's two more that won't carry off folks' chickens."

"I hear you boys got a silver fox." There was a suggestion of antagonism in Jack Mayhorn's voice as he said this.

"Yes," Johnny replied. "And we've still got him."

"Do you know, fellows," Jack gave vent to a chuckle that seemed a little strained, "back in Michigan, where I lived on the shores of Lake Superior, there was a feller who used to go lake-trout fishin'. He trolled with an out-board motor. Always got 'em, too, a whale of a fine catch.

"But you know," he edged forward in his chair, "there was net fishermen there, too. Fished fer a living. And one day when we was lookin' over this sportin' fellow's catch, the fish he claimed he'd caught trollin' we found had net marks on 'em."

"Net marks?" someone said.

"Sure." There was a shifty look in Jack's eyes. "He'd been liftin' nets an' helping himself to the fish that didn't belong to him. And I was wonderin'," he paused, "just wonderin', Johnny, if that silver fox of yours mebby had a lame foot or—or somethin'."

The silence that followed was painful. Johnny made no reply. His fingers worked along his palm, that was all.

It was Blackie Dawson who spoke at last. "I take it, Jack," he spoke slowly, "you are insinuating that these boys took the fox from your trap. Let me tell you, old man, that sort of thing calls for a fight; in the north it does."

Jack made no reply, but Johnny did.

"I'm sorry," he said, speaking slowly. "It doesn't mean a fight to me."

"You won't fight?" Blackie stared at him.

"Not to settle a personal grudge," Johnny replied slowly. "If Jack wants to think we took the fox from his trap, that's his privilege. If he would like to examine the fox that's his privilege also. But I'm not going to beat him up just to make him take back something he's said. That might seem to be a point of honor but we all have our own codes of honor. It may seem queer but I'd rather take an insult than give someone a beating."

"Take a beating you mean," Jack sneered. He was nearly twice Johnny's size.

"Joe," said Johnny, turning to the store-keeper, "you told me you got two pairs of boxing gloves through the mail."

"Sure, Johnny, I did. Here they are." Reaching behind him the store-keeper drew out two pairs of gloves.

"Put 'em on, Johnny," Blackie encouraged.

Put 'em on! Put 'em on!" came from all over the room. There was a stir of expectancy in the air.

"Sure, I'll put them on," Johnny grinned. "What do you say, Joe? I'll box you five rounds. Five friendly bouts for fun, money or marbles."

The crowd stared, Johnny was talking not to the man who had offered the insult but to his friend the store-keeper.

For a moment Joe stood staring at him. Then, as the light of a smile spread over his face, he said, "Sure, Johnny, I'll box you, not for money or marbles, but just, you might say, for fun."

It will be a long time before the settlers of Matanuska Valley will again witness such a match as followed. Five rounds for fun, between friends? Yes, perhaps. And yet there were times when even Johnny doubted that. True, he was not angry for a moment, just in there doing his best. But Joe? He was wondering about him.

Though he had told no one in the valley about it, Joe had, only the year before, belonged to the U. S. Marines. The Marines neither give nor ask quarters. And Joe had been champion of his regiment. As for Johnny, well you know Johnny. If you don't, you should have been there that night.

From the start it was leather against leather, a slap for the chin, a thrust at the heart, a bang on the side of the head, and after that a clinch.

Seldom had men been more evenly matched. Joe was older, more experienced, Johnny younger, faster on his feet.

They had not been going a minute when an involuntary ring had formed about them. In that ring, gaping open-mouthed was Jack Mayhorn.

Twice Johnny was down on a knee. Each time he was up and at it. Once, backed into a corner, Joe tripped and fell. He, too, was up before the count of three.

The fifth round was wild. Had there been an announcer, he must surely have lost his mind calling, "A right to Johnny's chin, a left to his ear. The ear is bleeding. Oh—a! A slam on the side of Joe's head that makes him slightly groggy. Johnny's following through. The clinch! The referee (Blackie) separates them. They are sparring now. Now! Oh, now! Johnny takes one on the chin. He's down. One—two—three—He's up again." So it went to the end.

As the cowbell, rung by young Larry Hooker, announced the close of the round, the crowd went wild with enthusiasm, but Joe, seizing Johnny by the glove, dragged him into the kitchen at the back of the store.

"Boy, you're a whiz!" he exclaimed. "There was a time or two when I thought you had me." He was mopping Johnny's face with a wet towel.

"Not a chance," Johnny laughed. "I didn't know what I was stepping into but I did my best."

"Listen," Joe held up a hand. The tumult in the outer room had died down. Blackie Dawson was about to make a short speech. "Gentlemen," he was saying, "the day after tomorrow at early candle light, there'll be another boxing bout in this room. It will be between—" he paused—"between Jack Mayhorn and—he—he has a choice—Johnny Thompson or Joe Lawrence."

"No!" a voice fairly roared after the shouts had subsided, "I got a bad foot. My footwork, it ain't no good at all." It was Jack Mayhorn who spoke.

"So it's *your* foot that's bad and not that silver fox's foot?" Blackie bantered.

The crowd let out a roar that could have been heard a mile.

"That'll about fix Jack Mayhorn," said Joe. "He's not likely to bother you much now."

An hour later, when the customers had "cleared out and gone home," Johnny and Lawrence found themselves in Joe's kitchen. Blackie and Joe were there. So was Mrs. Joe. They were all eating huckleberry pie and drinking hot chocolate.

"Johnny," said Joe, feeling a plaster on his chin, "why did you do it?"

"Do what?" Johnny stared.

"Pick on me for a fight. I never done you no wrong."

"That's why," was Johnny's astonishing reply. "It's an old Eskimo custom."

"What is?" They all stared at him.

"According to the Eskimo law," Johnny went on soberly, "if you are going to be killed it has to be done by a near relative or very close friend. So-o—" he added with a spreading grin, "I thought you'd do as well as anyone. And you did—even better."

"Anyway," Blackie supplemented after their laugh was over, "folks in Matanuska Valley will know who among us can put up a good scrap and that always helps."

When one is young he thinks only of the present and the future, never of the past. As the two boys walked home that night, they thought much of the future. The bond of friendship between them and Blackie Dawson was growing stronger every day. When spring came, would they go booming away with him on a Coast Guard boat in search of adventure in Bristol Bay? Who could tell?

In the meantime there was work to be done, plenty of it. Some twenty acres of land was yet to be cleared. In the spring stumps must be pulled. Without a tractor this would mean back-breaking labor.

"Perhaps we can get more foxes?" Lawrence said, thinking out loud.

"Yes, and other wild creatures," Johnny added. "That country 'back of the beyond' has never even been explored. There must be wild life back there that's never been seen. Peary found white reindeer on one of his expeditions. Who can tell what we'll come upon if we keep up our search?"

Who, indeed? The boy had spoken more wisely than he knew.

CHAPTER VI
SMOKEY JOE'S BLUE BEARS

Johnny awoke with a start. What had wakened him? He could not say for sure. He had a feeling that it had been a human voice, perhaps a shout.

Propping himself up on one elbow he listened intently. There came no sound save the long-drawn distant howl of a wolf. "Must have dreamed it," he murmured as he drew deep into the caribou-skin bed.

The night was cold, bitter cold. It was dark. Like chilled white diamonds, stars glistened in the sky. "What a change a few hours can make," he thought. They were sleeping in the mysterious Bill's shelter, he and Lawrence.

Why were they sleeping in this cheerless shelter? Warm beds awaited them at home. When one is young he does not need too good an answer for the thing he does. Both Johnny and Lawrence were born scouts. They loved the sharp tang of cold on their cheeks, followed by the quick glow of a campfire. The smell of wood-smoke, deer steak broiled over coals, dreamy hours just sitting before the fire, not talking, just thinking, all these were a joy to them. So they liked to get away for a night. Bill's camp was a convenient place.

Johnny did not fall asleep at once, instead his mind was crowded with dreamy thoughts.

Perhaps Bill was a gold prospector. Perhaps he had discovered gold. Then when he returned to this camp, they might all go tramping away to find the spot and stake out claims.

"That would ruin the settlement," he told himself. "People would desert their dreams of making homes for brighter, more illusive dreams of wealth. And yet—" What did he wish? He could not tell.

When they had retired for the night the moon had been shining, a bright fire gleamed before their shelter. Now all was gloomy and cold. Should he rekindle the fire? "No. Too chilly," he shuddered. "Wait till morning."

The days that had gone before had been uneventful ones. More and more he had come to realize that they must have a tractor. Long hours they had worked clearing timber. Brush was burned. But wood must be saved for fires, for buildings and fences. Every day saw larger piles of wood on the cleared land.

"With a tractor and a stout sled we'd have it hauled home in no time," Lawrence had said to his father. "Without it—"

"Wait a little longer," his father had counseled.

So they were waiting and tonight, sleeping in Bill's shelter, they were still waiting.

So Johnny thought and dreamed until at last he fell asleep.

Perhaps he slept an hour, perhaps less or more. Then he awoke with a suddenness that set his senses reeling.

"Law-Lawrence!" he shouted in wild consternation. "The bear! The bear!"

Something solid and heavy as a bear had landed with all but crushing weight on his chest. It still rested there but did not move.

"That's no bear," said a gruff, good-natured voice. "That's my pack. Sorry! Didn't know you was here."

"Lawrence!" Johnny exclaimed. "It's Bill!"

"Not Bill neither," the stranger disagreed. "They call me Smokey Joe."

"Smokey Joe!" Johnny peered into the darkness, trying to get a look at the man's face. "Smokey Joe. I've heard of you."

And he surely had. Smokey was a well-known character in the valley. The old-timers told how he came and went. Always in search of gold, he would disappear for months.

"Then," one of the motherly women added, "just when we think he's gone for good, up he pops again. We feed him up and patch his clothes. Then, like some boy, he's off again.

"But he's no boy," she added. "He came to Alaska in the gold rush of '97."

"Eighteen-ninety-seven!" Johnny had exclaimed. "More than forty years ago!"

"He never left," the gray-haired lady had added. "He came from the Cumberland Mountains somewhere and he still speaks in their queer way.

"They say," she added with a lowered voice, "that he struck it rich once, had nearly half a million dollars, and that he's got some of it hid away in the hills somewhere. But, then," she sighed, "you can't believe anything you hear and only half you see in Alaska. Alaska is a place of wild dreams."

Johnny was recalling all this as he made haste to split dry wood into fine pieces, whittle some shavings, then light a blaze in their out-of-doors fireplace.

"It's about morning," he said, at last looking into Smokey Joe's seamed face. "Did you come far?"

"Been travelin' mighty nigh all night," the old man drawled. "Me and my hounds here." He nodded at three powerful dogs, already curled up on the snow for a sleep. "Right smart cold up yonder. Hit's a sight better here in the bottoms."

"We'll have coffee before you know it," Johnny said cheerily. "Coffee and sour-dough flap-jacks."

"Ah," the old man sucked in his breath. "Sour dough flap-jacks. They shore do stick to yer ribs. Reckon Smokey Joe's the flapjack eatinest feller you almost ever seed."

Lawrence grinned. This old man spoke a strange language.

"A bear!" Smokey chuckled. "You all thought I were a bear! That's right smart quare."

"We almost caught a cub," Johnny explained. "Caught him alive, I mean."

"Almost." Lawrence laughed. "But his mother objected."

"Bears," said the old man, blinking at the fire. "Back thar in them thar glaciers thar's bears you might nigh wouldn't believe the plain truth about."

"Why?" Johnny sat up. "What's strange about them?"

"Might nigh everythin's quare, I reckon. Hm," the old man sniffed the coffee, "smells powerful good."

"It'll be boiled in a minute or two," said Johnny. "But tell me about those bears."

"They're blue, plumb blue, like a thin sky." The old man struggled for words. "They're right smart woolly like sheep, I reckon. But they ain't sheep. God-a-mighty, narry a bit of it. One of them clawed my lead dog like tarnation. An' they're the fish-eatinest critters you most ever seed."

"Polar bears?" Johnny suggested.

"Polar bears, big as good-sized hounds!" Smokey sniffed. "Who's ever hearn tell of sech polar bears?"

Who indeed? Johnny was growing excited and confused. "Woolly, blue bears no bigger than dogs," he was thinking. "What kind of bears could they be?"

In his confusion he upset the coffeepot and spilled half its contents. For all this, there was plenty left. Smokey Joe drank it piping hot, ate in a ravenous manner. Then, springing to his feet and calling to his dogs, declared he must get down to Palmer for a new pack of grub.

"He's found a trace of color in some dashing stream that doesn't freeze, not even in winter," was Johnny's conclusion. "He's going to hotfoot it right back and get rich—maybe."

"But, Johnny," Lawrence was not smiling, "do you really suppose there are any such bears as he described?"

"Of course not," was Johnny's prompt reply.

"But, Johnny, if there were, if we caught one alive! No bigger than a dog. We could do it, Johnny. We could buy a tractor."

"Forget it. It's all a pipe dream, I tell you."

But Lawrence did not forget Smokey Joe's blue bears, nor, in the end, did Johnny.

CHAPTER VII
A STRANGE BATTLE

Shortly after noon of that same day a slim, bright-eyed man in a huge beaver overcoat drove up to the Lawson cabin. Johnny and Lawrence, who were about to go back to their wood cutting, stared at him.

"Hello, boys," was his surprising greeting. "I hear you bring 'em back alive."

"Why, yes, we—Sometimes we do," Johnny replied in confusion.

"Blackie Dawson told me about you."

"Oh, Blackie." Johnny's face brightened.

"I am in the animal business," the man explained, alighting from his hired sled and allowing Lawrence to lead his horse away. "I thought you boys might help me a little."

"Help you? Oh, sure!" Things were looking better and better. "Here's where we get a start," Johnny was thinking.

"What have you?" the man asked.

"Well, er—mister—"

"They call me Professor Ormsby," said the stranger. "You may call me what you please."

"Well, then, Professor," Johnny went on, "we have a silver fox, a perfectly keen fox."

"Caught in a trap, I suppose?"

"No. By hand."

"By hand!" The Professor stared. "How do you do it?"

Johnny told him in as few words as possible and with no dramatics at all, just how it was done.

"Oh, I say!" the Professor exclaimed. "That's great! You took a chance with that fox. But, let me see—No-o, I can't use a silver fox. How about beavers?"

"We haven't taken any beaver. We—well, we were afraid it might be against the law even to catch them alive."

"I have a government permit," said the Professor. "But if you haven't any beaver—"

"Catching beaver would be easy. We have a grand colony not three miles away," Lawrence put in. "We might—"

"How about mink?" Johnny asked. "We have some fine ones. Or snow-shoe rabbits?"

"I suggest that you eat the rabbits," the Professor laughed. "I'll have a look at your mink. But beaver! There's your main chance. Can't you get me some? Big ones, the bigger the better.

"You see," he smiled, "we think we're really doing good through this work. In the big cities, hot in summer and cold in winter and crowded always, there are hundreds of thousands of children who would never know what a woodchuck, a monkey, a beaver or a bear looked like if they didn't see them in a zoo. Brings real joy to them, I'm sure. Many's the fellow who dates his first real interest in the wide out-of-doors to his visit at the zoo."

"Yes, I—" Johnny had scarcely heard him. "Could we do it?" he was asking himself. He was thinking of beaver. "Why not? Thousands and thousands of city children." His head was in a whirl.

"I think," he tried to make his voice seem very cheerful, "I think we can supply the beaver. Can't we, Lawrence?"

"What? Yes. Oh, yes," Lawrence replied.

"One of them must be a big one, a real boss of the village," warned the Professor.

"We've got him," Johnny laughed uncertainly. "Napoleon himself."

"Yes. Oh, yes. We've got him, all right," Lawrence did not laugh.

Strangely enough, as a short time later the boys went away on one more "Bring 'em back alive hunt" there was no spring in their step. Their faces were sober. If they succeeded this one more time, the coveted tractor would be within their grasp, and yet they appeared anything but happy.

"Might even get the Titan," Lawrence tried to tell himself. This boy loved fine machinery and that Titan tractor was a beauty. It had power, plenty of it. With it they could not only pull stumps and plow fields for themselves, but do work for other settlers on shares and, in quiet times, they could work on the road. "Four live beavers," he thought. "That's all it takes." Yes, that was all it took, and yet—

Up a small stream that flows into the Matanuska River early in the year the boys had discovered a beaver colony. Many an hour they had spent watching these busy beavers. Never in all their lives had they seen such feats of engineering done by creatures of the wild.

There were at least sixty beavers in the group. One big fellow, weighing sixty pounds or more, was the leader. He was the boss contractor. And such a boss as he was!

"Napoleon," they had named him. He stood for hours, as the great little general is pictured, straight, stiff and soldier-like. To him came the others. Were there trees to be felled? Two lieutenants came marching soberly up to him. They talked earnestly, nodding their heads, like real people, then off they rushed to start a dozen beavers doing the work.

It was so in everything. Most interesting of all had been the building of the big dam. This work, the boys understood, must be rushed. Winter would come. Ice would freeze two feet thick. The level of the stream must be raised to six feet so the beaver tribe could use the water beneath as a highway all winter long. The water must be dammed up.

This dam building, done under the wise direction of old Napoleon, had progressed rapidly for a time, then a sudden freshet of water loosened some of the beams and the whole affair threatened to go down stream.

"What'll they do now?" Lawrence had asked.

"Wait and see," was Johnny's answer.

Old Napoleon sent his men, like sub-engineers, all over the dam, making a study of conditions. Then, apparently abandoning all this work, he ordered a new dam built a hundred feet farther down stream.

But did he truly abandon his first work? Not a bit of it. He and his crew built just enough of a dam below to raise the water and relieve the pressure from the original dam. Then, with an air of professional pride, Napoleon returned to his old post and the work was well completed before frost.

"He," Johnny thought to himself, "is the friend we mean to capture and sell into slavery, Old Napoleon." Little wonder that his heart was heavy. "Old Napoleon," he whispered once again.

But what was this? As they neared the beaver colony where they were sure to find Napoleon out sunning himself, they caught sight of some creature skulking through the brush.

"It's a wolf," Johnny whispered. "Let's follow him."

Follow him they did, and to their consternation saw that he was headed for the beaver colony.

"We'd better frighten him away," Lawrence whispered. "He'll drive all the beavers beneath the ice. Then we won't be able to lasso a single one."

This, Johnny knew, was good advice, but for some reason scarcely known to himself, he said, "Let's wait."

When at last they caught sight of the beaver village, they saw old Napoleon standing stiff and straight as ever in his place. He was having a sun bath.

After sneaking along through the brush, the wolf made a dash at the beaver.

"He'll kill him," Lawrence whispered.

Did he? Strange to say, as the wolf came near, the beaver did not stir from his place. This appeared to surprise the wolf, who did not at once rush in for the kill. Sneaking up close, he made a dash at the beaver, but stopped just short of his goal. Still the beaver did not move. To the boys this seemed strange. Their respect for the old fellow grew by leaps and bounds. He appeared to be saying, "What's a wolf that one should fear him?"

"He—he's great!" Johnny shrilled.

"Magnificent," Lawrence agreed.

Snarling low, the wolf began dashing and snapping at the beaver. Each snap made him bolder. Now his ugly jaws were three feet from the apparently defenseless hero of wild life, who had decided to give his life for his home and his people. Now he was only two feet away. And now only a foot.

"We—we'd better step in," came from Lawrence.

"Wait," Johnny gripped his arm hard. Perhaps he should stop the wolf, but he waited, fascinated.

"Now!" Lawrence caught his breath. The end, he was sure, had come.

And then, of a sudden, things did happen, but not in accord with expectations. Old Napoleon had chisel-shaped teeth that cut wood like a hatchet. Without a sound, as the wolf, having grown bold, snapped in his very face, he shot forward to close those murderous teeth over the wolf's closed jaws.

"Great Scott!" Johnny muttered.

The struggle that followed was fast and furious. Kicking and scratching, the wolf rolled over and over, but not once did Napoleon's locked grip loosen. It was only when his opponent, completely exhausted and all but smothered, lay limp at his side, that he at last pried his own jaws apart to climb awkwardly to his place in the sun. Instantly the wolf dragged himself to his feet, to go slinking away into the brush.

For one full minute the boys stood there motionless. When Lawrence spoke his voice was husky. "Johnny, I've often suspected old Napoleon of being a tyrant. He's lazy, too. I've never seen him do a lick of work. But he is one swell engineer and a grand boss."

"What's more, he's no coward," Johnny added.

"Johnny, I can't do it," Lawrence dangled his lasso.

"Neither can I," said Johnny. "Let's go."

Turning, they made their way in silence down the narrow stream to its mouth. There they dropped down upon the snow to put on their skates.

"Johnny," said Lawrence, "we're a pair of old softies."

"That's right," said Johnny. "But I don't mind, do you?"

"Not a bit. Let's go."

"Get 'em?" the Professor asked as they came stamping into the cabin.

"No—er, well, no we didn't," Johnny stammered.

"How come?" the man's face sobered. "That was your big moment."

Sensing the tenseness of the situation, Mrs. Lawson said, "The coffee's hot. I have some spice cookies, just out of the oven. How would you like a bite to eat?"

"That—that would be splendid!" said the Professor.

When, over their cups of coffee, the boys had told the whole story, there was a strange look on the Professor's face as he said, "Can't say that I blame you. Under the circumstances I should have done the same thing. We shall be obliged to get our beaver some other way. And as for your tractor—"

"We—we'll manage," Lawrence replied slowly. Then, "By the way, Professor. You must know about bears. Are there any light blue bears?"

"Blue bears? Let me think! Oh, certainly! They belong up this way, too. Very rare they are, though."

"Blue bears!" Lawrence became greatly excited. "Small blue bears, no larger than a good-sized dog, with woolly hair? They—they live on fish?"

"What?" It was the Professor's turn to become excited. "You haven't seen one? You—you couldn't catch one for me, could you?"

"Sure—sure," Lawrence stammered. "No, I mean we haven't. That is, we could, I—I'm sure we could."

"If you were to bring me one of those bears alive and in good condition," the Professor spoke in a deeply solemn voice, "you might name your own price. Glacier bears, they are called. There is a stuffed specimen in the United States National Museum, but not a single living specimen in captivity anywhere."

"We—we'll hunt up Smokey Joe tomorrow," Johnny said. "He's seen them. He can tell us where they are. In fact, he told us all about them, only I thought it was all hooey."

"Smokey Joe? Who is that?" the Professor asked.

"An old prospector," Johnny explained. "He's been all over this country."

"In that case," said the Professor, "much as I should like a glacier bear, I suggest that you postpone your search until late spring. Those rare creatures inhabit the wildest sort of country, rocks, cliffs and glaciers. They are worse than mountain goats. You would almost certainly perish. And besides, it is fairly certain that they, like most others of their kind, hibernate. And so—"

"So another bubble bursts," Johnny groaned.

"Don't be too pessimistic," the Professor smiled. "I shall hope to hear from you sometime in June or early July. A single specimen will do.

"And, by the way," he added as he rose, "I've decided to offer you a hundred dollars for your silver fox. That may not seem such a good price, but is really above the market."

"Sold! Sold!" the boys exclaimed in unison. And so it was that the boys collected their first real money. They were, however, still a long way from their goal.

CHAPTER VIII
THE STORMY PETREL'S FIRST PRIZE

As the winter wore on the cold grew more intense. Ice on the streams was thick. Wild animals appeared to vanish from the scene. Snow covered much of the river surfaces. All these things served to make "bringing them home alive" more difficult.

At last the boys gave up this strange occupation and turned to the task of clearing the ten-acre tract.

"If we can get that tract cleared we'll plant it in barley, oats and peas. When these are ground together they make excellent chicken feed. We'll go in for poultry. There's a steady market for dressed chickens and eggs at Fairbanks," said Mr. Lawson.

"Yes, if we get that tract cleared," Lawrence thought, but did not say. No further suggestion that they go into debt for a tractor was made by anyone.

The long Arctic evenings were divided between games and dreaming. The fame of Johnny's and Joe's boxing had traveled far. The recreation room at Palmer was given over to this excellent sport two nights a week.

A boxing club was formed. Even Jack Mayhorn dropped his feud with Johnny and joined up. Members of a boxing club at Seward accepted an invitation for a contest. Johnny and Joe won this by a narrow margin.

On the evenings when business or pleasure did not take them to town Johnny and Lawrence might often be found dreaming by their own hearth-fire.

"When the land is cleared and plowed, when the grain is sowed and we've earned a breathing spell," Lawrence would say, "then we'll hunt up old Smokey Joe and go out for one of those glacier bears."

"If we can find Smokey Joe," Johnny would smilingly agree. "And if they don't need us for service in Bristol Bay."

"Bristol Bay," Lawrence would reply doubtfully. "Seems as if I'd rather catch animals alive than go after those Orientals."

"We'll take them alive, too," Johnny chuckled.

Lawrence was not so sure of this. Hour after hour Blackie Dawson, who had discarded his crutches, entertained them with stories of his adventures with the Orientals.

"They want everything for themselves. They spoiled their own fishing by catching the salmon before they were half grown and canning them right on the ships. Now they want to come over here and do the same, right up there in Bristol Bay.

"They catch our fish and can 'em, then they pop into Seattle or San Francisco and say, 'See all the fine fish we have canned for you. Come and buy them.'

"Think we'll do that?" he would storm. "Not on your life! We'll get 'em. You'll see.

"But the Shadow," his voice would drop, "that shadow that passes in the fog. How's a fellow to catch that? Who can tell? But we'll get it, too," he would add, striking the table a lusty blow.

In March he received his appointment as Commander of the *Stormy Petrel.*

"A swell boat." He was proud of her. "Come on down with me and we'll turn her motors over once or twice just to get the rust out of 'em."

Johnny and Lawrence accepted his invitation. They did far more than turn the motors over. With Lawrence as engineer and Johnny as first mate, they cruised for three days along the Alaskan shores.

On the third day, "Just to get in practice," as Blackie put it, they hailed a suspicious-looking craft carrying no flag. When the skipper failed to heed Blackie's command to head around, they sent a ball from their shiny brass cannon over her bow and she promptly hove to.

She was found to be carrying contraband drugs. "A fair capture in a fair chase," as Blackie expressed it. "A regular feather in our cap."

"Well," said Johnny, "how did you like it?"

"Those are glorious motors," Lawrence enthused. "How I'd love to be their master. But I hope—" he hesitated. "I rather hope we go after the glacier bears. That's the surest way to get a tractor. And a tractor's what we need most."

"Time and fate will decide," Johnny said soberly.

"Time and Blackie," Lawrence added with a laugh.

"And Smokey Joe," Johnny amended.

CHAPTER IX
FATE LENDS A HAND

Strangely enough it was Fate, in the form of an automobile accident in far away Seattle, that cast the final vote deciding their choice between the *Stormy Petrel* in Bristol Bay and a glacier bear hunt with Smokey Joe.

Spring had come at last. Steadfastly refusing to go in debt, the Dawsons, with Johnny's help, were attempting to clear their land without the help of a tractor.

At first it was fun. With blasting powder and dynamite they blew the larger stumps into shreds. The boom—boom—boom of blasts might be heard for miles.

There remained thousands of smaller stumps. To force these from the tough sod and heavy black soil with pick, shovel and bar, was back-breaking labor.

"Give me time," Johnny would groan when morning came. "There's a place in my back somewhere that bends. I'll find it. Just give me time."

Joke as they might, they could not but feel that progress was woefully slow and that seed-time would find them all unprepared.

One bright day an automobile came bumping over the uneven road to pause before their field. Out from it popped an old friend.

"Blackie!" Johnny exclaimed. "I thought you'd be in Bristol Bay by now."

"I'm on my way," Blackie puffed. "And so are you.

"Mr. Lawson," he exclaimed, "I must draft your boys into my service."

"What about these stumps," Mr. Lawson straightened his stiff back.

"What'll it cost to have 'em out with a tractor?" Blackie demanded.

Both Johnny and Lawrence looked at him with gleaming eyes.

"Why do you need my boys?" the man among the stumps demanded.

"Two of the men who were to accompany me have been crippled," Blackie explained. "They were in an auto accident in Seattle. I had a wire this morning. They were so badly hurt they could not let me know sooner. And tomorrow we were to sail. Already there has been news of trouble in Bristol Bay.

"I tell you, Mr. Lawson," Blackie was pleading now. "It's for Alaska and her greatest enterprise I ask it. Yes, and for every humble American who makes a simple meal from a can of salmon. As I see it, it's your patriotic duty to let them go."

Then Blackie did a strange thing for him. He quoted poetry—

"'Not once nor twice in our fair Island's story

Has the path of duty been the way to glory.'

"Mr. Lawson!" he exploded, "let them go. Here!" he waved a roll of bills. "I'll pull your stumps. I'll plow your land and sow your seed. Let them go."

Who could have refused? Surely not a man with Tom Lawson's patriotic soul. "Al-all right, boys," he said huskily. "Go get your clothes. And—and Blackie, I must trust you to bring them safely home."

"No need to worry," Blackie reassured him. "We'll all be back to shoot fire-crackers with you on the Fourth of July. And may your fields be green by then."

Twenty-four hours later Johnny and Lawrence found themselves standing on the narrow deck of the *Stormy Petrel* watching a familiar shore-line fade from their sight.

To Johnny this seemed just one more journey into the great unknown. To Lawrence it was something more, his first long trip away from his own family. Strange emotions stirred within him. Questions he could not answer crowded through his mind. How long was this journey to last? What strange, wild adventures would he meet? What would be the outcome? Would they be of some real service?

Through his thoughts ran Blackie's two lines of verse,

"'Not once nor twice in our fair Island's story

Has the path of duty been the way to glory.'"

What did it mean? He had only a vague notion.

"MacGregor," he said to the gray-haired engineer who thrust his head up from the engine room, "what do these words mean?" He repeated the lines.

"Well, noo, me lad," said the friendly old Scotchman, "I've never been too good at poetry. But it seems to me it says if ye think first of yer country and her needs, ye'll be likely to get the things you want most fer yerself; that is, I meant to say, in the end."

"Thanks." Once again the boy paced the deck. Was this true? He wanted a tractor, a humble, earth-digging, sod-plowing, stump-pulling tractor. It was a strange thing for a boy to want, he knew. Most boys would have wished for an automobile, but he wanted a tractor. Would he get it?

As they left Seward behind and headed west to follow the Alaskan Peninsula until they could cross over into Bristol Bay, it seemed to him that they were heading directly away from his heart's desire. The pay they were to receive was small. It would help very little. "And yet," he thought with a firm resolve to do his best in his strange new position, "Sometimes fate does seem to take a hand in making things come out just right. Here's hoping."

The *Stormy Petrel* was a sturdy boat with powerful motors. She was small— little larger than a good-sized speed boat. But how she could go!

There was a small after-cabin with six bunks ranged along the sides. Here George, the colored cook, presided over a small stove producing glorious things to eat. The coffee was always hot. And indeed it was needed, for, as a gray fog settled down upon them, the air became bitter cold.

Johnny was to take watch for watch with Blackie as steersman. Lawrence was to exchange watches with MacGregor and preside over the motors. Had this been a week's cruise simply for pleasure, nothing could have been more delightful. Johnny loved boats. Lawrence listened to the steady roar of his motors and was joyously happy.

And yet, there hung over them a sense of approaching danger.

"Say-ee!" Johnny exclaimed on the third day, after taking their position and studying the chart. "We're closer to Asia than we are to Seattle."

"Aye, that we are, me lad," MacGregor agreed.

"Yes, and that's why it's so easy for these Orientals to slip over here and trap our fish," Blackie exploded.

"And that," he went on quietly, "is why you settlers in Matanuska Valley are given so much financial aid. Your old Uncle Sam wants you there. He's going to locate more and more people along these Alaskan shores. You watch and see! Why? To give them homes? Not a bit of it. To have people here to watch those Orientals, that's why."

"Well," said Johnny with a laugh. "Looks like we'd learn a lot of geography and current history on this trip."

"No doubt about that, me lad," MacGregor agreed.

They had been on the water for five days when, touching Johnny on the shoulder, Blackie pointed at two spots of white against the sky.

"That's snow on two mountain peaks," he explained. "The cannery we're heading for is built on the banks of a small river close to these mountains. We'll be there before dark. And after that," he took a deep breath. "After that our real work begins."

"A new world," Johnny murmured dreamily.

"You don't know half of it," said Blackie. And Blackie was right.

CHAPTER X
A NEW WORLD

Next morning Johnny and Blackie Dawson sat on the deck of the *Stormy Petrel*. A wild nor'wester was whipping up the ocean spray. Even on the river well back from the narrow bay, little whitecaps came racing in.

"No day for going out!" Blackie grumbled. "Pile up on the rocks, that's what we'd do."

"Yes," Johnny agreed. Fact is, he at that moment was not thinking of the sea, but of the quiet Matanuska valley, of the snug home he and his people had built there. He wondered in a vague sort of way how far this, his latest venture, would lead him from that home. He was thinking not so much for himself as for his cousin Lawrence.

Strange as it might seem, the welcome given them by the people of the cannery had not come up to their expectations. Men had stared at them, had mumbled something under their breath, then gone about their work.

Work there was to be done, too. There was a pleasant hum of expectancy about the place. Every motor, machine and conveyor in the place was being given the once-over. Power-boat motors thundered as they went through their testing. Johnny felt a desire to become a part of it all. And yet—

"Fool sort of thing this rushing off after adventure," he told himself. But, had love of adventure alone brought them this far, hundreds of miles from his quiet valley? Love of home was one thing, love of one's country another. You didn't—

His thoughts broke off short. There had come the sound of a loud voice. The *Stormy Petrel* was anchored on a narrow dock that ran along the side of a long, low building, the cannery. A window was open. The speaker was near. Johnny caught every word. As he listened his ears burned. But what could he do? He was on his own boat. People who do not mean to be heard too far must speak softly.

Perhaps the man meant to be heard. There was more than a suggestion of anger and threat in his voice as he said, "Fine fix we're in! Huh! Here we are part of the biggest industry in Alaska. Fifteen million dollars a year. The Orientals start cuttin' in on us. We call for help, for protection. And what do we get? A lousy tub no bigger than a gill-net boat. And how's she manned, I ask you?"

A second voice rumbled words that could not be understood.

"She's manned by a crippled young skipper," the first speaker growled. "An old Scotch engineer and two kids. Protection! Bah!" There came a grunt of disgust. "We'll have to take things into our own hands."

At that a door slammed and they heard no more.

"Well?" Blackie tried to scare up a grin. It was not a huge success. "Kids," he said.

"We're not quite that," Johnny said quietly. "We *are* pinch hitters."

"Sure you are," Blackie agreed. "But I wouldn't trade you for half the so-called men in the regular service.

"Say, Johnny!" His voice dropped. "Know who that was talking?"

"No-o."

"It was Red McGee. He is the union agent that looks after the interests of these men working in the canneries. They say he's a good man and a fighter, but narrow. A—a fighter. Hm'm—" Blackie seemed to play with the words.

"Johnny," his whisper sounded like an exploding steam valve. "You *like* to box, don't you?"

"Nothing I like better," Johnny grinned. "Started when I was six and never stopped."

"Red McGee's a boxer," Blackie said. "Off times like this I'm told these men up here go in for boxing bouts. Nothing savage, you understand, just a few friendly rounds. And Red's never been beaten by any of them."

"And I suppose you expect me to trim him, at least to try it?" Johnny's face was a study.

"No-o, not just that, only a few friendly rounds. I'd like you to represent the *Stormy Petrel*."

"I think I get you," Johnny's lips moved in a quiet smile. "You want this crowd to know that I'm not a child."

"Johnny," Blackie's tone was almost solemn, "it's important. Mighty important! If this fishing mob gets started and if they find a ship out there in Bristol Bay catching fish contrary to law, there's going to be trouble. More trouble than all our diplomats can clear up in a year.

"There's no getting 'round it, this business has been slighted. But this much stands out like your nose—we've got to do what we can. And we can't do much if these Alaskans sneer at us.

"So-o, son," he drawled, "if they give you a chance tonight you step in. And if a chance doesn't open up, I'll open one.

"Come on," he sprang to his feet. "It's time for chow."

Passionately fond of boxing as Johnny surely was, he found himself dreading the encounter Blackie had proposed for that night. Why? He could not have told.

A strange audience awaited him in the long, low-ceilinged room where, on working days cases of salmon were stored for shipping. Seated on empty packing boxes, the men formed a hollow circle. This circle was to be the ring for the evening's entertainment.

"They're all here," Blackie grinned. "A dozen nationalities: Italians, Finlanders, Swedes, down-east Yankees, an Eskimo or two and what have you.

"One thing they've got in common," his voice rang true, "they're all Alaskans at heart. Hard fighters, straight shooters, they look you square in the eye and treat you fair. But when anyone tries any dirty, underhanded work, you'll see sparks fly."

"Well," Johnny smiled. "Whatever else happens, there will be no crooked work tonight. I don't fight that way."

"Don't I know it?" Blackie agreed.

"Well, now, here we are," he chuckled a moment later. "Reserved seats. Box seats, mind you. Who could ask for more?"

As Johnny sat, quite silent in his place, watching one short three-round match after another being fought in a good-natured rough-and-tumble fashion between boatmen, cannery workers, carpenters, engineer and blacksmith, he became more and more conscious of one fact—the crowd was holding back its enthusiasm.

"It's like the preliminary bouts in Madison Square Gardens," he said to Blackie at last. "They seem to be waiting for the one big fight. What's coming?"

"Can't you guess?"

"No-o, I—"

"It's you and Red McGee. They're waiting for that."

"What?" Johnny half rose to his feet.

"Keep your seat." Blackie pulled him down. "Ever hear of the grapevine telegraph?"

"Yes, in—in a sort of way."

"It's the mysterious manner in which news travels up here. These fellows know about you. The minute I gave them your name they busted out, 'The kid that packs a wallop?'"

"And you—"

"I said, 'Sure! None other. But does Red McGee know it?'

"They said, 'Guess he doesn't. He's been in Seattle, just come up.'

"Then I said, 'Mum's the word. We'll just ask him to give Johnny a few pointers in boxing.'"

"And they agreed?" Johnny seemed ready to bolt from the room.

"Sure. Why not?" Blackie grinned. "It's the grandest way to get in with all of 'em. They like a good joke. So does Red McGee."

"Even if it's on him?"

"Even if it's on him. Absolutely."

"Then he's a real sport," Johnny settled back in his place. "It will be a real joy to box him a few rounds."

"Okie doke," Blackie seemed relieved. "But, Johnny," he added, "pull your punches. Murder isn't legal in Alaska, not south of the Arctic Circle."

"I only hope Red McGee remembers that," was Johnny's solemn reply.

CHAPTER XI
THE FALL OF THE RED MCGEE

When by popular request, emphasized by loud shouts, Red McGee was called upon to put on the gloves, he stepped forward smiling. Johnny slid to the very edge of his box for a good look. This was the first time he had seen the man. He was a little startled.

"So that's what I'm going up against?" he murmured low.

Six feet of man, broad shoulders, a shock of red hair that stood straight up, a square jaw and glittering eyes, this was Red McGee.

And was he popular? The hoarse shouts of approval that made the rough rafters ring as he stepped out on the floor left no room for doubt.

Red was to box three rounds with a man named Tomingo, a dark-faced foreigner who piloted a gill-net boat. Johnny was thankful for this brief reprieve before he too should step into the ring.

That Red McGee was no mean boxer he learned at once. He had a head on his shoulders and a remarkable eye.

"He seems to anticipate every move this Tomingo makes," Johnny groaned in a whisper.

"They have boxed together before," was Blackie's answer. "Perhaps many times. When you play a game with a man many times, just any game, you come to know his tricks. But you, Johnny, he doesn't know you. It's an advantage.

"But, Johnny," he cautioned after a moment's silence, "don't let him get to you. Look at those arms! If he hits you just once, a good square one, you're sunk.

"And, boy," his voice dropped, "this is a big spot. It's important, mighty important. These fellows must respect us, have faith in the *Stormy Petrel* and her crew. If they don't, they'll go storming out there six hundred strong, looking for trouble. And if they find it! Oh, man! They might start a war."

"There!" Johnny breathed. "There's the bell. That match is over. And Red McGee is just nicely warmed up."

The tall, lanky boatman who acted as referee shuffled off the floor.

"Who's next?" Red McGee invited with a broad smile.

It was evident at once that few of the men cared to take him on. Tomingo was wearing a flaming patch where Red's glove had raked his chin.

"Red," one of his own men volunteered, "there's one of them kids from the *Stormy Petrel* who'd like to learn a little about boxing. Would y' mind a teachin' him?"

"One of those boys?" Red looked squarely at Johnny. Johnny flinched. Did Red know? "Oh, sure!" Red's lips spread in a broad smile. "I like boys, always have. Sure I'll show him.

"Look, Tom," he turned to the referee. "Help the boy on with his gloves. Be sure he gets 'em on the right hands. It's awkward boxing if you don't." He let out a low chuckle.

Once again Johnny flinched. What did Red know? Probably nothing. This was just his way of poking fun at the *Stormy Petrel's* crew. This made Johnny a little angry, but not too much.

"Show 'em, Johnny," Blackie hissed in his ear. Next Johnny found himself shaking the great paw of Red McGee. And so the fight began.

Nothing had been said about the number of rounds, nor their length. Johnny was a little taken back when the referee settled himself on a box in a corner.

"But then," it came to him with a sudden shock, "I'm supposed to be a learner. When you're taking lessons there are no rounds. Well, I'll be a learner, for a while."

He carried out his plan to the letter, almost. After giving him a few words of instruction, Red invited him to "Sail right in. Hit me if you can."

The boy did not exactly "sail in." Instead, he danced about the big man in an awkward but tantalizing fashion. There is nothing more irritating than a fly buzzing around one's head. Johnny was, for the moment, Red McGee's fly. He was here, there and everywhere. At times he appeared to leave himself wide open to one of Red's sledge-hammer blows, but none of these really connected.

All the time Johnny was thinking, "How long will he stand this? How long? How—"

The answer came sooner than he expected. His arms were all but at his side, he was looking Red squarely in the eyes when he saw those eyes change. It was like the change of a traffic light from green to red. Of a sudden, a huge gloved paw came squarely at the side of his head.

No one will ever know what that blow might have done had it arrived at its proposed destination. It did not arrive. Johnny's head was not there. Instead, it was Red who, to his vast surprise, received the lightest of taps on the tip of his chin.

The crowd saw and roared. There were men, plenty of them, who knew that, had Johnny not pulled that punch, Red would have hit the floor.

Did Red know? For the life of him Johnny could not tell. One thing he did know, this was no longer a boxing lesson, nor was it to be a sparring match. It was instead to resemble an old-fashioned fight with no gong, no referee and no time out. Red McGee was aroused. There could be no doubt about that.

Johnny kept his opponent going about the ring in a whirl. Twice he stopped and all but fell into Red's waiting fists. Twice he heard the whistle of a glove as it brushed his ear.

Once, when he was in Blackie's corner, he heard a hoarse whisper, "Steady, there, boy. I can't afford to lose you."

Once, in a mad rush, Red McGee tripped, falling to his knees. Backing away into a corner, Johnny gave him time to regain his feet. Gladly would the boy have remained in that corner for the count of a hundred. All too soon he caught Red's challenge.

"Come out an' box."

"Red's in a tight place," Blackie said in a low tone to Lawrence. "I'm almost sorry I got him into it. He's got a bull by the tail and can't let go. If he quits now he's afraid he'll lose the respect of his men. If he goes on, well, anything may happen."

In the end two things happened. Both were surprises to Johnny.

The older man was tiring. Johnny found that by using a little strategy he could tap the man's chin at will. Be it said to his credit, he tapped that round red chin only twice. There is little to be gained by an unnecessarily large score.

Those two taps, little heavier than love pats, stirred up something deep in Red's nature. His men were looking on a new man. Not that they thought the less of him for it. Rough and ready men of the northern wilds, they understood as few ever do.

Then things began to happen fast. Red lunged at Johnny. The boy dodged. The man came at him again. In one of those seconds when reason goes on a vacation, Johnny tried one more pulled punch to the chin. He did not pull it fast enough. Red McGee fell upon that punch as a polar bear falls upon a spear.

There came a resounding thwack. Then, doubling up like an empty sack, Red McGee spread himself neatly on the floor. He was out for much more than the count of ten.

The hush that followed was appalling. But the shout that followed! Nothing Johnny had ever before heard even remotely resembled it. Perhaps a gladiator in the Roman Arena, had he returned from the dead, might have recognized it with joy or fear.

In vain did Johnny try to analyze that sound. Was it a cheer? Or was it a curse? Should he be carried out like a football hero or crushed by an infuriated mob?

Strangely enough, as he stood there half paralyzed by the sudden shock of it all, he was conscious of one voice. Above the shout had risen a woman's scream. And he had not known there was a woman in the place. Who was she? Where had she come from? Why was she here?

"It's all right, boys," he heard a big voice boom. "He didn't aim to do it. He pulled his punch. Twice he did it. He—"

The speaker broke off short. There was a girl at his side, or perhaps a young lady. Johnny was not sure. A round, freckled face and angry eyes, that was all he saw. In another second she would have been at him, tooth and nail. But the big foreman, who had done the talking, wrapped a long arm about her waist as he said, "It's all right, Rusty. Everything is O. K., child. He didn't aim to do it. An' your daddy ain't hurt none to speak of. It's what they call a knockout. He'll be 'round in a twinkle."

At that the girl hid her face in the foreman's jacket to murmur fiercely, "The brute! The ugly little brute!"

And Johnny knew she meant him. Because she was a girl, because he had hurt her and he felt miserable, he slipped back into the outer fringe of the milling throng.

CHAPTER XII
A PTARMIGAN FEAST

As Red McGee opened his eyes he found the foreman, Dan Weston and his daughter, Rusty, bending over him.

"Wh-what!" he exclaimed, struggling to a sitting position, "what in the name of—"

"You fell into a fast one, Red." The foreman laughed. The crowd joined in this laugh but not the girl. Sober of face, she stood looking down at her father.

"Daddy," she began, "are you—"

"Do you mean to say that kid from the *Stormy Petrel* put me out?" Red McGee interrupted.

"Well, you went out," the foreman drawled. "The boy was the only one near you so I reckon—"

He was not allowed to finish for at that Red McGee let out a tremendous roar of laughter.

"Ho! Ho! Ha-ha-ha!" he roared. "That's one on Red McGee."

"But, boys!" he struggled to his feet. "I want to admit right here. There might be something to that *Stormy Petrel* crew after all. Give 'em a chance, I say."

"Sure! Sure!" the crowd boomed. "Give 'em a chance."

"Where's that young roughneck?" Red demanded, staring about him. "I want to shake his hand."

"Here—here he is!" Blackie pushed Johnny forward.

"I—I'm sorry—" Johnny began.

"Young man," Red McGee broke in, "never apologize. Your enemies don't deserve it, and your friends don't demand it. From now on we're pals. Shake on it." Their hands met in the clasp of a grizzly and a bear cub.

"What's more," Red went on, "the treat's on me. You're coming up to dinner with me, all four of you fellows from the *Stormy Petrel*. Ever eat ptarmigan pot pie?"

"Never have," said Johnny.

"Well, you're going to before this day is ..."

*   *   *   *   *   *   *   *

... look into her eyes, he found himself seeing cold, blue-gray circles expressing as near as he could tell, undying hate.

"Of course," he said to Blackie, "you can't expect a girl to understand about boxing, with all of its ups and downs. But it does seem she might give a fellow the benefit of the doubt."

"She will, son. She will," Blackie reassured him. "Perhaps sooner than you think." Was this prophesy or a guess? Time would tell.

Rusty McGee was the type of girl any real boy might be proud to call a pal. With an easy smile, a freckled face and a mass of wavy, rust-colored hair, she caught your interest at a glance. The strong, elastic, healthy spring of her whole self kept you looking.

More than once during his visit to the McGee summer home, a stout log cabin nestling among the barren Alaskan hills, Johnny found his eyes following her movements as she glided from room to room.

"Boy, she can cook!" Blackie exclaimed as he set his teeth into the juicy breast of "mountain quail," as ptarmigan are often called. And Johnny did not disagree.

Since the crew of the *Stormy Petrel* were her father's friends, it was evident that Rusty meant to do her best as a hostess. But to Johnny she gave never a smile.

"How she must love that old dad of hers!" Blackie whispered once. Johnny's only answer was a scowl.

Yes, Johnny was shunned and slighted by this youthful "queen of the canneries," as she had once been called, but the *Stormy Petrel's* engineer, old Hugh MacGregor, came in for more than his full share of interest.

Hugh MacGregor was truly old. His thatch of gray told that. With grandchildren of his own he was just a big-hearted old man. Rusty was not long in sensing that.

When the dinner, a truly grand feast, was over, the others, Blackie, Red McGee, Lawrence and Johnny retired to the glassed-in porch where they might have a look at the barren hills of Alaska and the wide, foam-flecked sweep of Bristol Bay, and, at the same time, talk of fish, Oriental raiders and the sea.

MacGregor remained behind to "help with the dishes."

"Do you like Alaska?" Rusty asked him.

"Oh, sure I do!" was the old man's quick response. "I spent a winter much further north than this many years ago. I was quite young then. It was thrilling, truly it was. Cape Prince of Wales on Bering Straits—" his voice trailed off dreamily.

"Way up there?" the girl exclaimed. "What were you doing?"

"Herdin' reindeer and Eskimo," he laughed. "I crossed the straits in a skin boat with the Eskimo and lived a while in Russia without a passport. You do things like that when you are young.

"Ah yes," he sighed, "youth is impulsive, and often wrong." He was thinking of Johnny. He knew how Johnny felt about things. He had become very fond of the boy.

Did Rusty understand? Who could tell? Burying her hands in foamy suds, she washed dishes furiously. Nor did she speak again for some time.

Meanwhile, over their pipes, Red McGee and Blackie were discussing the task that lay before them.

"I suppose you know all about this Oriental fishing business," Red suggested.

"I'm not sure that I do know all about it," was Blackie's modest reply. "Suppose you tell me."

"It's like this," Red cleared his throat. "There was a time when we thought the salmon supply off these shores was inexhaustible. We caught them in nets and traps just as we pleased.

"Then," he blew out a cloud of smoke, "there came a time when we woke up to the fact that the whole run of salmon might vanish. You know what that would mean?"

"Yes, I know," Blackie agreed. "The little man in Hoboken, Omaha and Detroit who hasn't much pay and has a big family could no longer feed the children on a fifteen-cent can of salmon."

"Right," McGee agreed. "More than that, thousands of fine fellows, just such men as you saw tonight, fair-minded, honest men that would," he paused to chuckle, "that would see one of their best friends knocked cold by a stranger in a fair sparring match and not want to kill him, men like that would be out of a job. Their families would go hungry. You know, about all they understand is salmon catching."

"And so?" Blackie prompted after a moment's silence.

"So the government and the canners got together on a conservation program; so many fish to be caught each year, the same number allowed to go up stream and spawn.

"The plan was well worked out. We've put the salmon industry on a sound foundation. It will continue so for years unless—"

"These Orientals are allowed to come over here and set three-mile-long nets across the bay," suggested Blackie.

"That's just it!" McGee struck the table a resounding blow. "They're taking advantage of a technicality of international law. And unless we drive them out—"

"Not too loud," Blackie cautioned. "There goes one of them now."

"What?" McGee sprang to his feet. A slender, dark-haired person was passing down the path before the cabin.

"No," he settled back in his place. "He's not one of 'em. He's one of our Eskimos. We have three of them down here. It's a little off their regular beat. But they are keen at locating the runs of salmon. Inherited it from their fathers, I—

"But say!" his voice rose. "He does look like one of those Orientals."

"Sure he does," Blackie agreed.

"We might use him for a sort of spy," McGee's voice dropped to a whisper. "His name's Kopkina. Used to work in a restaurant. He picked up the Oriental lingo, at least enough to pass for one of 'em. If some of them come around here, we'll have Kopkina mix in with them. He might find things out, important facts."

"It's a good idea," Blackie agreed.

"Yes," MacGregor was saying to Rusty, as he told more of his adventures in the very far north, "it was a bit peculiar goin' up there like that, livin' with the Eskimos. And me still a young fellow like Johnny Thompson now." He shot her a look. She smiled at him in a peculiar way, but said never a word.

"It was the food that was strange," he went on after a chuckle. "Of course, you can chew polar bear steak if you've got uncommon good teeth. Seal steak's not half-bad and reindeer makes a grand Mulligan stew."

"Yes, I know," the girl agreed. "We have some reindeer meat sent down every season. Stay with us and you'll have a taste of it."

"We'll stay, all right," MacGregor declared. "That's what we're here for to stay, hunting Orientals and shadows—shadows." He repeated the word slowly. "Blackie believes in moving shadows in the fog on the sea."

"Shadows?" the girl stared at him.

"Sure! He says they glide along across the sea with never a sound. Like some phantom schooner it was," he said.

"That's strange." The girl's eyes shone. "There was a gill-net fisherman last season told something just like that. He was an Italian, sort of a dreamer. We didn't believe him. But now—what do you think?"

"I don't know what to think," MacGregor scratched his gray thatch.

"But, Mr. MacGregor," the girl said after a moment, "didn't you have a thing to eat except Eskimo food?"

"What? Oh, yes, up there, up there when I was a kid same as Johnny," MacGregor laughed. "Sure—sure we did. It came on a sailin' schooner all in cans.

"We had evaporated potatoes and eggs in cans, butter pickled in cans, hot dogs in cans, everything. And the Eskimos," he threw back his head and laughed. "They'd stand around watchin' to see what we'd take out of a can next.

"And then we got a phonograph," he laughed again.

"A phonograph?" Rusty said.

"Sure. First one those little brown boys ever seen. Had a long tin horn to it, that phonograph did. The Eskimos looked at it and tapped the tin horn. They said, '*Suna una?*' (What is it?) We didn't tell 'em, so they tapped it some more and said, 'All same tin can-*emuck.*'

"Bye and bye we cranked it up and started it going. The record was a white man singin' 'Meet me in Saint Louis, Louie. Meet me at the Fair.'

"Well, that was funny!" he chuckled. "The Eskimos just looked and listened for a long time. Then one of them looked at the others and said, 'Can you beat that! A white man in that tin can!'"

The merry laugh that rang out from the kitchen was heard by those on the porch. Johnny heard it with the others and was glad—glad that that fine girl could laugh even if it wasn't his joke.

"See that cannery out there?" Red McGee was saying. "Cost a cool million dollars. Paying interest on the investment, too. Also it's giving two thousand people a living. But these Orientals with their floating canneries—"

"Floating canneries?" Lawrence broke in.

"Sure! That's what they've got. They pick up some big hulk of a ship cheap, install some canning equipment, load on a drove of cheap coolies and steam away. Pretty soon they're over Bristol Bay, just off the shores of Alaska, but beyond the three-mile limit. Three miles! Bah!" he exploded.

"I'm in favor of calling every square mile of Bristol Bay American waters," Blackie replied.

Red McGee stared at him with sudden approval. "Say!" he roared, "we must be brothers."

"We ought to run those Orientals off," Blackie grinned. "We're here to start just that. That boat of ours may not seem so hot, but she's got speed and power, three airplane motors in her. Good ones, too. Once we sight an Oriental fishing boat setting nets too close behind the fog they're coming ashore."

"To do a lot of explaining."

"Yes, and for quite a long visit."

"That's the talk," Red McGee stood up. "Here's hoping the wind drops so you can get there. The fishing hasn't really started. No foreign boats have been seen. But they're there. They made a haul last year. We're sure of that. So why shouldn't they come back?"

"Why not?" Blackie agreed.

In all of this time neither Johnny nor Lawrence said a word. For all that, they were thinking hard and their young hearts were on fire with a desire to do their bit for the good old U. S. A. and Alaska, their present home.

"Nice place you've got here," said MacGregor, as he joined the party on the porch.

"It will pass," was Red McGee's modest reply. "I built it for my wife. She loved these rugged hills and the smell of the sea. She—" his voice faltered. He looked away. "She left us a year and a half ago. But Rusty and I, we—we sort of carry on.

"But if those Orientals—" his voice rose, "Oh! Well, enough of that for today. It's good of you fellows to join us in a feast!"

"It's been swell!" said Blackie.

"Swell! Grand! Mighty keen!" were the impulsive comments of the boys.

"We know each other better," said Blackie.

"A whole lot better," Red McGee agreed.

"Goodbye, Rusty," MacGregor called back through the house.

"Goodbye! Goodbye! Come again soon," came back in a girlish voice.

"I wonder," Johnny thought as he took the winding path leading down to the wharf. "Wonder if we'll ever get to come back here?"

CHAPTER XIII
THE SHADOW

"Fog." There was more than a suggestion of disgust in Johnny's tone as he said this word. It was the next morning. After a good night's sleep aboard the *Stormy Petrel* he felt ready for anything. The moment he awoke he had listened for the pounding surf.

"Gone!" He had leaped from his bunk. "Storm's over. Now for a good look at Bristol Bay and perhaps, just perhaps, some of those Orientals."

"Here's hoping," Lawrence agreed.

Yes, the storm was over, but here instead was a damp, chilling blanket of dull, gray fog.

"Can't see a hundred feet," he grumbled.

"You'll get used to that, son." It was Red McGee who spoke. He had been leaning on the rail talking to Blackie. "'Men and Fog on the Bering Sea.' That's the name of a book. And it's a good name. There are always men and nearly always there is fog.

"Fish are coming in," he added as a cheering note. "Two boats are just in from a try at the gill-nets. They made a fair catch."

"But this fog," Johnny insisted, "gives those Orientals a chance to slip in close, doesn't it?"

"It does!" Red agreed. "Blast their hides! That floatin' factory of theirs comes in close to the three-mile limit. Then their other boats, small, fast ones, can come over the line and set nets. You couldn't see them in the fog. They'd put 'em up early. Three miles of nets.

"Claim they're catchin' crabs. Crabs, me eye!" he exploded. "Crab nets are set on the bottom. Salmon nets are set close to the top. Drift nets are what they use. We've never found one inside the three-mile line, but we think they've been there all the same.

"If you ever do find one," he turned to Blackie, "take it up and bring it in. We'll can their fish an' boil their nets.

"Shouldn't be any three-mile line," he continued. "All our shore water belongs to us. So do the fish. It's food, son! Food for the millions. And these Orientals would have had fish on their own shores if they hadn't exterminated them."

"We're going out right now," said Blackie. "Going to have a look for that shadow that passes in the fog. We've got a nice swivel cannon up there forward. Don't know whether you can hit a shadow, but it won't do any harm to try."

"All the same, this *is* a serious situation," said Blackie as they headed out into the fog. "These Alaskans are a strange people. They are like the men of the old west, the west that's gone forever; fearless men with hearts of gold, fighting devils when they know they've been wronged. And this Oriental raiding business is an outrage, providing it's true."

"But is it true?" Johnny asked.

"That," said Blackie, "is what we're going to find out.

"Johnny," he said after a moment, "go up forward and remove that box. Let our little brass messenger swing with the boat."

A moment later, up forward, a small swivel cannon swung from side to side. As it did so it seemed to point, first right, then left.

"This way or that?" Johnny thought. "I wonder which it will be."

Hour after hour the fog hung on. Hour after hour Johnny squinted his eyes for some moving object in that blanket of gray fog. The cold, damp ocean air chilled him to the bone. Stamping his feet, he held doggedly to his post. When his watch was over he went below to soak in the heat of the stove that George, the colored cook, kept roaring hot. He drank two cups of scalding black coffee, downed a plate of beans and a whole pan of hot biscuits, then spread himself out on a cushioned seat to close his eyes and dream.

In those dreams he saw creeping gray shadows, darting fish and a pair of laughing eyes. The eyes closed. When they opened the face wore a frown.

"Rusty!" he whispered. "Wonder if she'll ever forgive me?"

All too soon his turn at the watch came. The days were long, twenty hours from dark to dawn. By nature a hard driver, inspired by his desire to help the Alaskans, Blackie steered his small craft endlessly through the gray murk.

Then—of a sudden Johnny rubbed his eyes—stared away to the right— closed his eyes—snapped them open again to whisper hoarsely,

"Blackie! The shadow passes."

"The shadow! Where?"

The boy's hand pointed.

"As I live!" Blackie muttered.

A short, slim line, little darker than the fog, moved slowly across the spot where sky and sea should meet.

"Ahoy, there!" Blackie roared. "What boat goes there?"

No answer.

"I'll show them!" Blackie put out a hand. Three powerful motors roared. The *Stormy Petrel* lurched forward, all but throwing Johnny into the sea.

Sudden as the movement was, it proved too slow. Like a true shadow, the thing vanished into the murk.

"It—it went down," Johnny stammered. "Must have been a whale."

"Or a submarine," Lawrence suggested.

"It did not go down," said MacGregor. "It slid away into the fog. And it was not a whale. I've seen plenty of whales. They're never like that."

"Wait!" Johnny sprang for the cannon. "I'll give them a shot just to let them know we're after them."

"No! No! Not that!" MacGregor waved him back. "'Speak softly and carry a big stick.' That was Teddy Roosevelt's motto. The grandest president that ever lived. There's time enough to make a noise after we've got 'em under our thumb."

"I—I'm sorry," said Johnny.

CHAPTER XIV
A VOICE IN THE FOG

Forty-eight long hours the *Stormy Petrel* haunted the gray fog. During far more than his fair share of that time, eyes blinking but tireless, Johnny stood on deck studying the small circle of black waters.

Three times his heart leaped as a dark bulk loomed before them. Three times he heaved a sigh of disappointment.

"Only one of the gill-net boats returning to the cannery," was the answer.

"They're running strong," was the joyous report of one fisherman. "Full load first trip. Looks like a grand season."

"Poor luck," came from the second. "We tried hard. Got only half a load. Have to come in anyway. It's the rule. Fish must always be fresh."

The third boat had had even worse luck. It was going back all but empty.

"No new calico dress for Nancy this time," the youthful skipper groaned.

"No gitta da dress," his Italian companion agreed.

At last, out of gas, with her crew half-blind from watching, the *Stormy Petrel* headed for the harbor.

"They're out there somewhere," Red McGee insisted, as he met them at the dock. "Must be anchored up north of here somewhere. It's the boys who go up that way who come back half-empty.

"But the wheels are turning," he added with a touch of pride. "Ever see a cannery in operation?" he turned to the boys.

"No, never have," was the quick response.

"Rusty," said Red, turning to his daughter, "how'd you like to show these boys through our plant?"

Did Johnny detect a frown on the girl's face? If so, it was gone like the shadow of a summer cloud.

"Sure! Come on!" she welcomed. They were away.

Somewhere Johnny had heard that a fish cannery was a place of evil smells and revolting sights. Dirty coolies gouging into half-rotten fish—that was his mental picture.

A surprise awaited him. Not a coolie was in sight. The place smelled as fresh as a May morning. To his ears came the sound of rushing water.

"Where are the coolies?" he asked a man beside a machine.

"This is him," the man chuckled. "An iron coolie."

As the two boys watched they saw the machine seize a large salmon, sever its head and tail, remove the scales and fins, clean it and pass it on in a split second.

"Jimminy crickets!" Lawrence exploded. "And I used to think I was the champion fish cleaner!"

Rusty favored him with a gorgeous smile.

When, a little later, Johnny made a try for that same young lady's smile, the cloud once again passed over her face, but no smile. He was not, however, entirely discouraged. It was, he thought, more as if she could not forgive him than that she did not want to.

"We saw the shadow pass," Lawrence confided to the girl, as at last they stood before a canning machine.

"Oh!" the girl breathed. "Did you? And what—"

"It vanished into the fog."

"I have a small motor-boat," the girl said, in evident excitement. "It's the *Krazy Kat*. I—I'm going out to look for the shadow in the fog."

"You—you'd better not do that," Johnny spoke before he thought. "You'd be—" He did not finish.

"I was practically born and raised here." She spoke to him, as an old-time Alaskan might to a newcomer.

Johnny did not resent it. He had spoken out of turn. And yet he was disturbed. He did not care to think of this fine young creature out there in the fog alone. Supposing she did find the Orientals setting nets. Suppose they found her, alone out there in the fog?

"None of my business," he told himself fiercely. "Just none at all."

The *Stormy Petrel* remained an entire day in port. Blackie spent his time listening to reports from the various fishing grounds. The shores of Bristol Bay are hundreds of miles long. Next time he went out he wanted to go to the right spot, if there were such a spot.

Johnny made the acquaintance of Kopkino, the Eskimo. From him he learned much about salmon, Orientals and the shores of Bristol Bay. And then, just at midnight, he passed the sturdy little man standing beside a dark pathway. There were three little men with him and they were all talking. They were not Eskimos. He was sure of that. But they were Orientals. He had heard enough of the languages to know.

At once his mind was filled with questions. Was Kopkino betraying his employer for Oriental gold, or was he acting as a spy for his big white brother? Who could say?

"He's an Oriental," Johnny told himself. "All Eskimos are. But after all—" He came to no conclusion.

Just before dawn the *Stormy Petrel* crept out into the fog. She was bound for an unannounced destination.

"Action," Johnny said to Lawrence. "This time we are to have action. I feel it in my bones."

One thing puzzled Johnny not a little. They were provisioned as if for a long trip, two weeks or more.

Several hours later the *Stormy Petrel* was once again circling about in the fog.

"Seems like it'll never end, this fog," MacGregor said to Johnny. They were on deck working out their watch. "Looks as if nature was on the side of those Orientals.

"Orientals," he continued musingly, "I don't suppose they're much different from the rest of us, only just some of them."

"Just some of them," Johnny agreed, giving the wheel a turn.

"Come to think of it," MacGregor went on, "there are a few white men who are not so honorable."

"Quite a few," Johnny agreed.

Truth is, Johnny was dead tired. He wanted nothing quite so much as to crawl into some warm corner and sleep for hours and hours.

"I don't hate them all the same," MacGregor squinted his eyes to look through the fog. Then he demanded low, "Hear anything, Johnny?"

"Not a thing."

"Thought I heard a voice coming out of the fog."

For some time after that neither spoke. They were listening with all their ears for some sound that might tell them the mysterious moving shadow was about to pass.

"What is this shadow?" Johnny asked himself. "Submarine, some fast, silent craft, or a whale?"

He liked the idea of a submarine. The Orientals had them. Why not use them for laying nets? Easy enough to vanish when danger was near.

"Hate, me lad, is destructive," the aged man's voice was solemn as he took up the thread of conversation he had dropped. "Hate destroys you as well as the people you hate."

He broke off short to cup a hand behind his ear.

"There *was* a voice," he insisted in a hoarse whisper.

"Yes, I heard it," Johnny replied, tense with sudden excitement.

Ten minutes had passed. They were beginning to relax when the sound came again.

"Over to the right," MacGregor shrilled. "Turn her about quarterin' them. Give her top speed."

"Right." Johnny twisted the wheel. The motors roared. It was a bold step that might have led to disaster. Should there be a boat out there setting nets, and should they crash at that speed, what would it mean? Johnny did not dare to think.

"There!" MacGregor gripped the boy's arm.

"Oh—ah!" Johnny groaned. "We missed them."

It was true. Off to the left, for the space of seconds, they saw an unmistakable dark, gray bulk. And then it was gone.

"Our own speed defeated us," declared MacGregor. "Ah, well, better luck next time."

"Or worse," Johnny grumbled.

Had he but known it, it was to be worse, much worse.

"As for me," MacGregor said a half hour later, resuming his talk, "I don't hate anybody. It's not worth while. Sometimes I hate the things they do. Mostly, I try to think of good people and the good things they do.

"And that," his voice rose, "that's what I like about this job of ours. If we can drive these Orientals from our shores we'll be doing good to our own people, a whole lot of 'em.

"Know what I see when I'm tired and I close my eyes?" he asked suddenly.

"No. What?" Johnny grinned good-naturedly.

"Children," MacGregor said in a mellow tone. "Children playing before an open fire and their mother puttin' the crust on an apple pie in the kitchen. And those, Johnny, are the children and wives of men way up here scoutin' around in the cold and fog for salmon. We're servin' them, Johnny, or at least we're trying to."

Just then Blackie's head popped up out of the hatch.

"See anything?" he demanded.

"Plenty," said Johnny.

"Yes, an' heard 'em," MacGregor added.

They told Blackie what had happened.

"So you think you heard them?" he asked.

"Think?" MacGregor roared. "We *know* we heard 'em."

"Might have been a seal barking to his mate, or mebby a loon. You can't be sure. Question is, if they're here, where's their nets?" Blackie came up on deck.

"Turn the boat north by east," he said to Johnny. "We're going in for a rest."

"Rest? What's that?" Johnny opened up a grand smile.

"Something we don't have much of," said Blackie. "But this fog burns your eyes. You're no good when you've been out too long.

"There's a cabin on shore if only we can find it," he explained. "A trapper's place, snug and warm. Red McGee told me about it. Trapper's gone south with his furs. We're to make ourselves at home."

Make themselves at home they did. After tying the *Stormy Petrel* up at a narrow dock they helped George up to the cabin with kettles, pans and food supplies. Then, while a jolly wood fire roared in the huge stove made of a steel gasoline barrel, laid on ends, they sprawled out on rustic chairs to sniff the odor of roasting beef and baking pies and to dream dreams.

With his eyes closed, MacGregor was seeing "children and their mothers putting the top crust on apple pies." In his dream Blackie held a struggling Oriental by the collar of his coat and the seat of his trousers. As for Johnny, he was seeing a round, freckled face all rosy with smiles. Then, to his dismay he was seeing that same face take on a somber look.

"Rusty," he thought once again. "Will she ever forgive me?"

The feast George had prepared was one fit for a king or even a big league baseball player, and the sleep they had in that cabin resting among the bleak Alaskan hills was the soundest Johnny had known for many a day. Well it was that this should be, for Fate had much in store for him.

CHAPTER XV
A ROAR FROM THE DEEP

"It will be an hour or two before I can get out," Blackie said next morning, standing up to stretch himself before the fire. "I want to go over some maps Red McGee gave me. Lawrence can draw up a simple chart that will keep us going right.

"MacGregor," he turned to the aged Scotchman. "How would you like to take Johnny for a circle or two in the fog? You might discover some evidence. It's nets we want most. If we can discover some of those nets inside the three-mile limit it will help a lot."

"Like nothin' better," said MacGregor. "Come on, Johnny, let's get goin'."

MacGregor had spoken for both of them. Johnny was fond of the engineer. He was old, mellow and kind, was MacGregor. This, he had confided to Johnny, was to be his last year with the service. Another twelve months and he would be pensioned. "And, Johnny," he had added, "I'm as eager as any boy to have a part in something big before I am compelled to go."

"I hope you can have," had been Johnny's heartfelt wish.

So now, with the sun still low and the fog, it seemed, thicker than ever before, they slipped out of the snug little natural harbor into the great unknown that is any sea in time of fog.

Standing at the wheel, Johnny watched the dark circle of water about them. Ever they moved forward, yet never did this circle grow larger. It was strange.

There was life at this circle. Now a whole fleet of eider-ducks, resting on their way north, came drifting into view. With a startled quack-quack they stirred up a great splatter, then went skimming away.

And now a seal with small round head and whiskers like a cat came to the surface to stare at them.

"Not worth much, that fellow," was MacGregor's comment. "Not much more hair than a pig.

"But look, Johnny!" his voice rose. "There's a real fur seal. His hide's worth a pretty penny. Wouldn't have it long either, if those Orientals sighted him. We used to have a hot time with 'em over the seals. Had to pay 'em to get 'em to leave the seals alone. That was a shame. Have to do the same with the salmon, like as not. We—

"Look, Johnny! What's that?" His voice suddenly dropped to a whisper, as if he believed the fog had ears. "Right over to the left, Johnny. Ease 'er over that way."

"Another seal," said Johnny.

"It's no seal," MacGregor whispered. "Johnny!" His whisper rose. "We got 'em. It's a net marker. Inside the three-mile limit. An' it's none of Red McGee's net markers either."

"That—that's right," the boy breathed.

"And there's the floats, Johnny! There they are!"

Sure enough, leading away into the fog was a wavering line of dots.

"We'll follow it," was MacGregor's instant decision. "See how much net there is, then—"

"I'll follow it," Johnny agreed.

"Set the boat to go five miles an hour. I'll time you." MacGregor pulled out his large, old-fashioned watch. "Now we'll see."

For a full ten minutes, in silence, the two of them watched the apparently never-ending line of net floats appear and disappear into the fog.

"Near two miles of it," MacGregor growled. "And yet no end. No wonder some of our fine boys come in with empty boats. These Orientals, they just find a place outside where the salmon run an' head 'em off. They—

"Slow up, Johnny!" he warned. "There's the end. Shut off the motor."

The motor ceased to purr. Silence hung over the fog. A seal bobbed up his head, then ducked. A large salmon, caught in the net close to the surface, set up a feeble splatter.

"Ease about," said MacGregor. "I'll pick up that net with this pike pole.

"Now," he breathed, leaning far out over the rail, "now I got her. Now—"

He had succeeded in getting his hands on the marker when catastrophe came thundering up at them from the deep. A tremendous explosion sent the water rocketing toward the sky. The prow of the *Stormy Petrel* rose until it seemed she would go completely over.

Frantically Johnny gripped the wheel to save himself from being plunged into the icy water. But where was MacGregor?

For ten tense seconds the boat stood with prow in air. Then with a slow, sickening swash, she came down.

"MacGregor!" Johnny cried. "What happened? Where are you?"

"Here—here I am!" MacGregor's voice rose from the sea.

"Johnny!" his voice was hoarse with emotion. "Shove off that life boat. Get her off just any way. There's a terrible hole in the *Stormy's* side. She'll sink in another minute. For God's sake, be quick!"

Johnny was quick and strong. If ever his strength stood him in good stead it was now.

The life boat hung over the afterdeck. The knots of ropes that held it in place were wet and stiff with fog.

"No time," he muttered. With his knife he slashed away the ropes. The boat fell on deck with a thud. It was a heavy steel boat. To his consternation, he saw that it had fallen squarely between the heavy rails. The prow must be lifted. Creeping under it, he put all the strength of his back against it. It rose.

"Now!" he breathed. "Now! And now!"

The boat was on the rail. He could fairly feel the *Stormy's* deck sinking beneath him. She was doomed, there was no doubt of that. Those heavy motors would take her down fast.

Once again he heaved. The life boat was now a quarter over the rail, now a third, now half.

Leaping from beneath it, he executed a double movement, a shove and a leap. He was in the life boat. The life boat plunged, all but sank, swayed from side to side, then righted herself.

There was a low, sickening rush of water. Johnny looked. The *Stormy* was gone. In her place were swirling water and in the swirl an odd collection of articles; a coat, a cap, a pike pole, and MacGregor's checkerboard.

"MacGregor!" Johnny called hoarsely. "MacGregor! Where are you?"

"Here! Over here!" was the cheering response. "I had to get away. She would have sucked me down."

Seizing an oar, Johnny began sculling the boat. In a moment he was alongside his companion. A brief struggle and MacGregor, watersoaked and shivering, tumbled into the boat.

"John—Johnny," his teeth were chattering. "There—there shou-should be d-d-dry clothes in the stern."

Dragging a half barrel from the prow, Johnny pulled out shirts, underclothing, trousers, socks and shoes.

"Seems you were looking for this," he chuckled as he watched the plucky old man disrobe himself.

"Johnny," said MacGregor. "In the Coast Guard service you are always looking for it an' all too often you're not disappointed."

When, a few minutes later, after a brisk rub-down, MacGregor had struggled into dry clothes and had succeeded in lighting his pipe, he said, "Well, me boy, we thought we had 'em an' now they've got us. We're miles from anywhere in a fog. And that's bad! Mighty bad."

"Do you suppose Blackie heard it?"

"What? The explosion? 'Tain't likely. We're all of four miles from there. Don't forget, we followed that net two miles. An' that explosion was muffled by the water.

"An' if he heard," he added after a brief pause, "what could he do? He's four miles away. No compass. An' no boat except maybe a fishing skiff. No, Johnny," his voice sounded out solemn on the silent sea. "For once in our lives we are strictly on our own, you and me.

"Well, me lad," he murmured a moment later. "They got us that time. Attached some sort of bomb to their net, that's what they did. Safe enough in a way, too, for how you goin' to prove it was their net? Yes, they got us. But you wait, me lad, we'll be gettin' them yet."

CHAPTER XVI
LOOMING PERIL

Many times in his young life Johnny had been on his own, but never quite like this.

"Not a bit of good to row," was MacGregor's decision. "We've not the least notion which way to go. If there was a breeze we might row by that. There's no breeze."

"No sun, moon or stars, either," Johnny agreed.

For a full half hour they sat there in silence. Off in the distance a seal barked. Closer at hand an eider-duck quacked to his mate. A sudden scream, close at hand, startled them for an instant. It was followed by a wild laugh. They joined in the merriment. It was only a loon.

There came a wild whir of wings. A flock of wild ducks, flying low and going like the wind, shot past them.

"That's north," Johnny exclaimed. "They're going due north to their nesting place. That's east," he pointed. "All we have to do is to row that way. We'll come to land."

"If you kept your course, which you couldn't," MacGregor chuckled.

"It's worth trying. Anyway, I'm cold," Johnny began to row. "There may be other bird flights to set me right."

There were not, at least not for fifteen minutes. When at last a pair of loons with long necks stretched straight before, passed them, to his disgust, Johnny saw that the boat was headed due north.

"Well," he sighed, dropping his oars, "At least I—"

"Listen!" MacGregor put up a hand.

Johnny listened. "Say! That's no seal."

"Nor a bird either. That's a human sound."

"Like someone trying to start a motor."

"Just that."

For a time the sound ceased. Then it began again.

"Over to the left." Once again Johnny took up the oars. This time he rowed slowly, silently. No telling whose motor had stalled. Fisherman, trapper, or Oriental? Who could tell?

Four times the sound ceased. Four times Johnny's oars rested on the surface of the water.

When, at last, a small, dark spot appeared on the surface of the sea, Johnny fairly ceased to breathe.

"Heck!" said a voice in that fog.

"Doesn't sound like an Oriental," Johnny whispered.

"Fisherman nor trapper either," replied MacGregor.

Leaning even more gently on his oars, Johnny sent his boat gliding forward. Then, of a sudden, he dropped his oars to stare.

"It's that girl, Rusty," he whispered hoarsely.

"The same," MacGregor agreed.

There could be no doubt about it. The girl was bending over to give her flywheel one more turn. Over her boy's shirt, high boots and knickers she had drawn a suit of greasy coveralls. On her face, besides a look of grim determination, there was a long, black smudge.

"Heck!" she exclaimed once more.

"Havin' motor trouble?" MacGregor spoke aloud.

The girl started so suddenly that she all but lost her balance. Then, after a brief spell of unbelieving silence, she said, "It's you, Mr. MacGregor! How glad I am to see you! I've been lost for hours. I—I went out to hunt the Shadow, that shadow you know. My motor's stalled. But now—"

"Now we're all lost together," MacGregor chuckled.

To Johnny, the girl gave never a second look.

"Do—do you suppose you could start it?" she said to MacGregor, nodding at her motor.

"No harm to try. At least we'll come aboard for a cup o' tea," MacGregor chuckled.

Johnny rowed the lifeboat alongside the girl's boat, the *Krazy Kat*, and they climbed aboard.

"She's not gittin' gas," said MacGregor, after he had turned the motor over twice.

"I know," the girl's brow wrinkled.

Without saying a word, Johnny scrambled back to the box covering the gas tank. After lifting the box off, he struck the tank a sharp rap. The tank gave off a hollow sound.

"You might try putting some gas in your tank," he said with a sly grin.

"Oh, but there must be gas!" the girl exclaimed. "There must be."

"Perhaps," said Johnny. "But it's empty. May be a leak." Drawing a small flashlight from his pocket, he bent over and examined the offending tank.

"Yep," he said, "there is a leak, a small hole, but big enough. Your gas is in the bottom of the boat, along with the bilge water. Any reserve supply?"

"Not a bit."

"Well, then, here we are." Johnny took a seat. "Now we have two boats and there are three of us. The motor-boat won't go, but—"

Suddenly he sprang to his feet. "You'd have a compass, wouldn't you?"

"Ye-es," the girl replied with evident reluctance, "but it—it's out of order. That's why I got lost."

"Well, anyway," Johnny said with forced cheerfulness, "now there are three of us. Two's company and three's a crowd. I always have liked crowds. Besides," the corners of his mouth turned up, "you've got something of a cabin."

"Oh, yes." The girl seemed, for the moment, to forget that she was speaking to one who had knocked her beloved daddy out. "Yes, there is a cabin. There's a small stove and—and some wood. There's tea and some pilot biscuits."

"A stove, wood, tea and pilot biscuits?" Suddenly MacGregor seized her and waltzed her about in a narrow circle. "Rusty, me child, you are an angel."

A half hour later found them comfortably crowded into Rusty's small cabin. They were sipping tea and munching hard round crackers.

"The fog'll lift after a while," MacGregor rumbled dreamily. "We lost our boat. That's bad. But there's marine insurance. That's good. We'll have another boat. I wonder," he paused to meditate, "wonder what Blackie and the others are thinking by now."

"And doing," Johnny suggested uneasily.

"Yes, and doin'," MacGregor agreed.

A half hour later, growing restless, Johnny crept from his corner, opened the cabin door and disappeared up the narrow hatch.

Ten seconds later he poked his head into the door to exclaim in a low, tense voice, "MacGregor, come up here quick."

MacGregor came. The girl came too. For a full half minute the three of them stood there speechless. They were looking up and away. Their eyes were wide and staring.

"MacGregor," Johnny asked, "what is it?"

"A ship," MacGregor whispered. "A thunderin' big ship. She's not two hundred leagues away. She's not movin', just driftin'. That's how she came close to us."

"Wha-what ship is she?"

"Who knows, son? But I'd lay a bet I could guess the country she came from."

"So—so could I." Johnny's throat was dry.

"We—we," Rusty pulled her old sou'wester down hard on her head, "we'd better get into the life boat and row away. It—it doesn't matter about the *Krazy Kat*. It really doesn't." She swallowed hard.

"We can try it," MacGregor agreed. "But I'm afraid it's too late."

"Well," he added with a low, rumbling laugh. "We were lookin' for 'em. Now we found 'em, we don't want 'em. Come on, an' mind you, never a sound!"

CHAPTER XVII
TRAPPED

"It's no use. We're in for it." Five minutes later MacGregor dropped his oars. From some spot close to that dark bulk against the sky had come the throb of a motor.

"Rusty, me child," the old man's voice was very gentle. "Be sure those golden locks of yours are well tucked in. Whatever you do, don't remove that sou'wester. For the present you are a boy. You must not forget."

"I—I won't forget." Rusty's fingers were busy with her hair.

"I only hope," the old man added soberly, "that my guess is wrong."

Scarcely were the words out of his mouth when a smart little motor boat, bright with red and white paint, hove into view. And on the deck, scarcely less smart in brass buttons and braid, stood a small man with slanting eyes.

Those eyes appeared a trifle startled at sight of MacGregor. "A thousand pardons." The little man's voice was smooth as oil. "What is that which you wish?"

"Only a few gallons of gasoline," said MacGregor.

The lightning change on the little man's face was startling. It was as if a dagger had suddenly flashed from his belt, yet his tone was smooth as before.

"Ah! You are out of gas? Very unfortunate. Your line, please. We shall escort you to our ship."

"But we don't want to go to your ship," MacGregor protested. "All we want is gas."

"Ah, yes, a thousand apologies. But here there is no gasoline, only at the ship. Your line, please."

"Say, you—" Johnny's angry voice was stopped by a heavy pressure on his arm.

"Give him our line, son," said MacGregor.

Grudgingly Johnny obeyed. A moment later, with the two boats in tow, the bright, little craft went rolling back toward that broad, black bulk.

"It's no use to quarrel with 'em," MacGregor said in a sober whisper. "We've fallen into their hands. I think that chap recognized me. I've been along the Pacific waterfronts for many years. So have these Orientals."

"But—but what will happen?" Rusty asked.

"Who knows?" was MacGregor's sober reply. "Let us hope for the best. They'll not let us go now. When they're well beyond the three-mile limit they may give us gas and let us go.

"In the meantime, Rusty," he warned, "don't forget you're a boy. It's a good thing you've got on knickers instead of a dress."

They were brought alongside. A ladder was let down. They climbed aboard. There they were ushered before one more small man who wore even more brass and braid. Johnny thought with a touch of humor that he would make a very fine monkey if only he had a cap, a tin cup and a string.

When MacGregor requested that they be given gasoline and allowed to leave, there were excuses, very profuse and polite, but quite formal. There were reasons, very unfortunate reasons; too much fog, a storm coming up, too few men to spare even one or two, to find the way alone quite impossible. Oh, quite!

The man, who beyond doubt was the captain, talked on and on.

It all ended by the *Krazy Kat's* being hoisted on board, by the little party drinking very black and very hot tea with the much adorned captain, and at last by their being escorted, for all the world as if they were embarking on a long voyage, to a pair of staterooms on the second deck.

For a time after the stateroom doors had been closed the surprised trio stood staring first at one another and then at their surroundings.

The two staterooms were joined by a door. There were two berths in each stateroom. There were round portholes, no other windows.

"That will be your stateroom, Rusty," MacGregor opened the door to the one beyond. "Keep your outside door locked.

"One thing more," hesitatingly he produced a pair of scissors, "I always carry them," he explained. "A man doesn't live everywhere as I have done, not in Alaska, without learning to cut hair. I'm a fair hand at it. Rusty, me child, those rusty red locks of yours have got to come off."

Without a word the girl dropped to a stool beside the berth.

"Johnny," said MacGregor, "I suggest that you step outside and stand guard. Don't leave the door, not more than three steps. If anyone comes near, make some noise on the door."

"Right," said Johnny.

"Rusty," said MacGregor, "do you ever box?"

"Oh yes, often." The girl's face flushed. "Often. Daddy and I box by the hour." She gave Johnny a strange, fleeting look.

"Good!" MacGregor exclaimed low. "Tonight we'll have an exhibition match, just you and Johnny. Two boys showing these Orientals how to play.

"And now," he nodded his head toward the door.

Johnny opened it ever so softly, peered through the crack, and was gone.

At the same moment the old man lifted the shabby sou'wester from the mass of lovely hair, blew on his scissors, heaved a heavy sigh, then slashed with apparent ruthlessness at a great handful of perfectly natural, copper-colored curls.

A half hour later the door opened a crack.

Taking the cue, Johnny stepped inside. He stopped short when he looked at Rusty.

It was with the greatest difficulty that he suppressed a smile at what he saw. The sou'wester was no longer needed. Good old MacGregor had done his work well. Rusty's hair looked like a real boy's.

"What a grand boy!" Johnny thought. And after that, "What a perfect brick of a girl she is!"

"Mac," he said a moment later, "there are twenty thousand fine big red salmon up forward. I stepped around a hatchway far enough to see."

"Twenty thousand," the old man murmured. "Our boys get fourteen cents apiece just for catchin' 'em. Twenty-eight hundred dollars. A grand livin' for two happy families. And that's the first haul. There'll be many another unless someone stops 'em.

"And we won't stop 'em," he added with a touch of sadness. "Not just yet. But you wait!" he sprang to his feet. "We'll get a break yet."

CHAPTER XVIII
FIVE ROUNDS AND A FRIEND

It may seem a little strange that MacGregor and his young companions accepted the whole situation so calmly. Yet the old man had lived long and in many places. He was wise in the ways of the world. He realized that they had already seen too much to be released at once. How long would they be detained? To this question he could form no answer. Perhaps until the end of the legal fishing season, twenty or more days away. Perhaps longer. They might even be taken to the Orient. After that some fantastic story might be told of their being picked up adrift on the high seas.

Johnny was thinking along these same lines. But he, unlike MacGregor, was already laying plans for escape. For the present, however, he was willing to bide his time.

Dinner was brought to them by a smiling little brown man. It was not a bad meal, as meals go on the sea—boiled rice, baked salmon and tea.

When it was over, MacGregor slipped out into the gathering night. While he was gone not a word was spoken. Johnny was busy with his own thoughts. So, he supposed, was the girl who now looked so very much like a boy.

He was thinking, "I wonder if there were shadows passing us in the fog. Or did we imagine them?" Certainly he had seen nothing resembling a shadow here. And this girl. Would she forgive him? Well enough he knew that in trying times such as these people were either drawn closer together or driven farther apart. He could only wait and see.

"There's hope in the airplane that young Dan MacMillan is bringing up," he thought with fresh courage. "If only he'd arrive and fly over this ship we'd manage somehow to signal him and then the whole navy would be on this old freighter's heels."

He was thinking now of something told to him in secret by Red McGee. He had been speaking of the cannery. It had been built by old Chad MacMillan. A crusty, honest, fair-dealing man, he had managed it for many years.

"Then he died," Red had gone on, "and young Dan MacMillan, just out of university and full of big ideas, inherited it. This winter I suggested that he hire a seaplane to go out scouting for these Oriental robbers.

"'It's a fine idea,' he said to me. 'A grand idea. I'll buy a seaplane and learn to pilot it. You'll be seeing me up there scouting around as soon as the salmon season opens.'

"That's what he said to me," Red McGee had drawn in a deep breath. "These wild young millionaires! What can you expect? He's not here now and like as not won't show up at all."

"What can you expect?" Johnny was thinking over his words now. "If only Dan MacMillan showed up over this old craft all these little brown men would be scared out of their skins."

But would he come? He dared not so much as hope.

He wondered about Lawrence and Blackie. He suffered a pang because of Lawrence. What a shame that he had dragged the boy up here! He would be far better off in Matanuska valley planting turnips and potatoes, hunting wild geese, and, perhaps, catching a glacier bear way back in the mountains.

But here was MacGregor. And he carried in his hands, of all things, two pairs of boxing gloves. Johnny had wondered where they were to come from, but now here they were.

"These little brown boys go in strong for boxing," the old man explained.

"I told them," continued MacGregor, "that you were one of America's most promising young boxers, but a little out of training."

"Quite a little," Johnny agreed.

"I said you and your boy pal would put on an exhibition match on deck tonight."

Rusty shot him a look, but said never a word.

"I hope you understand," the old man said soberly, "that I am asking you to do this for your own good." He was talking to Rusty.

She bowed gravely. Then, of a sudden, her face brightened. "I hope they take us lightly," she said. "That may give us a chance to escape."

"That's what it will," MacGregor agreed. "And this boxin' stunt is just the thing to put them off their guard."

A half hour later, beneath a brilliant electric light, with a circle of dark faces about them, Johnny and Rusty shook hands for the first time in their lives, then drew on the gloves.

Johnny had boxed strange people in many an out-of-the-way place. Never before had he boxed with a girl. He was not sure he was going to like it now. But with MacGregor as manager of the strange affair, there was no turning back.

It *was* strange, there was no getting around that. A swaying light, a host of sober, brown faces, the gray fog hanging over all, made it seem fantastic indeed.

There were to be five short rounds with MacGregor keeping time.

At the very beginning, Johnny discovered that his opponent was fast and skillful. Having no sons, Red McGee had taken it upon himself to train his daughter in the manly art of boxing. Life on the bleak Alaskan shore was often dull. The girl had welcomed each new lesson. And now Johnny was discovering that her punches that from time to time reached his cheek or chin, were far from love pats. They really stung, nor, try as he would, could he entirely escape them.

"She's taking it out on me because of her father," he thought grimly. "Well, I can take it."

What did the audience think of this affair? Who could tell? They watched in silence. Once when Rusty was tossed into their midst they helped her to her feet and pushed her into place. Their movements were so gentle, the flitting smiles about their lips so friendly, that, for the moment, the girl forgot her role and said, "Thank you."

The rounds passed speedily. When the fourth and last was up, Johnny said in a whisper, "Come on, Rusty, let's make this one snappy. Give them a real show."

Snappy it was. From the moment MacGregor gave them the signal they whipped into it with a wild swinging of gloves. Rusty's footwork was perfect. Johnny found himself admiring the manner in which, hornet-like, she leaped at him for a sharp, stinging blow, then faded away.

Perhaps he was admiring her too much. However that might be, in the last thirty seconds of the bout he stepped into something. Trying for a bit of reprisal in the way of a tap on her chin, he left an opening far too wide. Rusty's eyes opened wide, her stout right arm shot out and up. It took Johnny squarely under the chin and, "believe it or not," he went down and out like a match.

He was not out long, perhaps eight seconds. When at last his stubborn eyelids opened he found himself looking at a circle of grinning brown men and at Rusty who stood staring at him, but not smiling at all.

"Well," he laughed, "that must square the McGee's with Johnny Thompson."

"John—Johnny, please!" she cried. "I didn't mean to. I truly didn't."

"All right." Johnny sprang to his feet. "Shake on it. Let's always be friends."

The girl made no response. There was no need. She did clasp his hand in a grip that was friendly and strong.

A half hour later they were having one more cup of tea in their staterooms and Johnny was thinking, "Life surely is strange. I wonder how this affair will end."

Before he fell asleep he went over it all again. Blackie and Lawrence, the silent, moving shadow, the hard-working men on shore, the airplane that might come. When he was too far gone in sleep to think clearly he fancied that he felt the ship's propeller vibrating, that the ship was on the move. He was not sure. After all, what did it matter? There was nothing he could do about it. And so, he fell fast asleep.

CHAPTER XIX
ORDERED BELOW

Back in the trapper's cabin Blackie was in a rage. He stormed at the Orientals, at MacGregor, then at himself. From time to time he rushed out on the small dock in a vain attempt to pierce the thick fog and to listen with all his ears.

"The robbers have got them," he muttered. "I should have known. That shadow! It's done for them and for the *Stormy Petrel.*"

As night came on he settled down to sober thinking. "There's a fishing skiff out there by the dock," he said to Lawrence. "We'll have to put it in the water and make a try for the mainland. This cabin is on an island. Mainland must be thirty miles away. We'll make it. We'll find some sort of power boat. And then, by thunder! Things will get to popping!"

Lawrence, too, was disturbed in his own quiet way. He knew a great deal about Johnny. Many a time Johnny had been in a tight spot. Always, somehow, he had come out safely. MacGregor was old and wise. And, after all, this was not a time of war. Why need one worry too much?

There were a number of tattered books on the shelf in the corner. Evidently this trapper was something of a naturalist, for five of these were about animals and birds. In browsing through these, the boy made a real find, a picture of a glacier bear, a brief description, and the history of the animal as far as known.

It was with the feelings of a real discoverer that he read those words over and over. When he had finished he said to himself, "If ever I see one of those bears I'll know him."

But would he? At the present moment those bears seemed as far away as the moon. And yet, who could tell?

At dawn next morning the three of them, George, the cook, Blackie and Lawrence, carried their few supplies down to the dock, tacked a note on the door, climbed into the broad, clumsy skiff and rowed into the fog.

"We'll follow the shore as far as we can," said Blackie. "We'll have to cross a broad stretch of open water, but I think I can manage that with my pocket compass."

When at last Lawrence saw even the small island disappear from sight, he regretted the circumstances that appeared to make it necessary to leave that comfortable retreat.

When Johnny and his friends came on board that same morning, they found the fog still with them, but it was thinner. There was a suggestion of a breeze in the air.

"Going to clear," was MacGregor's prophecy. This, they were soon to discover, did not concern them too much, at least not in the immediate future.

When they had eaten a strange mixture of rice and meat and had gulped down some very bitter coffee, a little man with neither gold nor braid on his uniform came up to them, saluted in a careless manner and said simply, "Come."

They followed him from one deck to another until they found themselves in a vast place of steam and evil smells.

When their eyes had become accustomed to the light and steam, they saw long rows of men toiling and sweating over apparently endless tables. Before the tables, on a conveyor, thousands of large salmon moved slowly forward.

"No iron coolie here," Johnny chuckled. "Everything is done by hand. Heads off, tails, fins, all with big knives."

"Please," said the little man. He was holding out a long, thin, oilskin coat. Understanding his wish, Johnny put it on. Still wondering, he watched MacGregor and the girl follow his example.

"Please," said the little man again. "A thousand apologies." He was holding out three long, sharp knives, at the same time pointing with his other hand at a break in the solid line of salmon workers.

"Why, the dirty little shrimp!" Johnny exploded. "He wants us to go to work."

"Steady, son," MacGregor warned. "They understand English. I fancy there are worse places than this on the ship. We have no choice but to obey."

Johnny muttered, but dropped into place to slash off a large salmon's head.

He had worked in a rebellious humor for a quarter of an hour when, on looking up, he discovered that Rusty was performing the most disagreeable task in the salmon line. She was cleaning the fish. Shoving past MacGregor, he turned her half about as he muttered low, "You take my place."

To his great astonishment, he felt the girl whirl back to her place, give him a hard push, then saw her resume her work.

For a space of seconds he stood there stunned. Then he laughed low. The girl was wise, much wiser than he had known. She was supposed to be a boy. Boys were not gallant to one another. She would play the part to the bitter end. Johnny returned to his task.

"Mac," he was able to whisper at last, "why would they do this to us?"

"You answer," was the old man's reply. "Sh-sh—" he warned. "Here comes a big shot, one of the monkeys with gold buttons."

As he passed the "big shot" smiled suavely at them, but said never a word.

CHAPTER XX
A BATTLE IN THE DARK

Even at lunch time the toiling trio, Rusty, Johnny and MacGregor, were not invited to have their lunch on deck. Instead, they were served, like the coolie with whom they toiled, with great bowls of some mixture that looked like soup.

"Hm," MacGregor sighed, "fish chowder. And not bad."

Rusty's eyes shone. "What a lark!" She laughed outright. "I only wish we had a camera. My crowd down in Seattle won't believe me."

Johnny looked at her in surprise and admiration. "Here's one girl with a spirit that can't be broken," he thought.

"Reminds me of a time I was on the Big Diomede Island on Bering Straits," said MacGregor with a rumble of merriment. "We were cutting up a big walrus. I saw an old woman working over the stomach of that walrus. Know what the walrus lives on?" he demanded.

"Clams," said Johnny.

"Right. Bright boy," said MacGregor. "The thing that had happened was this. The walrus had been down to the bottom. He'd ripped up the sand at the bottom of the sea. He'd cracked a lot of clams and had swallowed 'em. He hadn't digested 'em yet when we shot 'im. Know what that Eskimo woman was doing?"

"Can't guess."

"She had a white pan and was savin' the clams from the walrus' stomach. And that night," there came a low rumble from deep down in MacGregor's throat, "that night we had seal steak and clam chowder for supper. An' I took seal steak."

"O-oh," Johnny breathed.

"Mr. MacGregor," Rusty said with a gurgle, "you wouldn't spoil anyone's dinner, would you?"

"Not for the world," was the old man's solemn avowal.

"Listen," MacGregor held up a hand. "I hear an electric generator going. It's on this deck. I wonder why? I'm going for a little walk."

"They'll chase you back."

"That's all they can do." He was away.

"The ship's beginning to sway a little," Johnny said. "Shouldn't wonder if we'd get a storm." The girl could not suppress an involuntary shudder.

"Johnny," she leaned close to speak almost in a whisper. "When we used coolie labor I learned to talk with them a little. I've been talking to the coolie who cuts off fish's heads next to me. He says they expect to have a boatload of fish in a week or ten days. Then they'll go back to the Orient."

"And if we go with them?" Johnny breathed.

"I've seen pictures of the Orient." The girl's eyes were closed. "It's gorgeous. It truly must be."

"Do you think we'd get to see anything?"

"Why not?" the girl laughed low. "It's all there to see. At least they can't keep us from dreaming."

"No, they surely cannot." At that Johnny did some very choice dreaming, all his own.

He was wakened from these dreams by the return of MacGregor. "It's the strangest thing!" he exclaimed. "I got a look into that place. There's a huge generator an' it's chargin' batteries."

"Batteries!" Johnny exclaimed in surprise.

"Sure! Banks and banks of large batteries."

"When submarines go under water," Johnny spoke slowly, "they use batteries for power. What do you think?"

"I don't think," said MacGregor. "Anyway, here's our little boss. He wants us to resume our duties as first-class cleaners of sock-eyed salmon."

As the day wore on Johnny watched Rusty ever more closely. The heavy, unpleasant work, together with the ever-increasing roll of the ship, was telling. He was not surprised that, after the day was over and they were allowed to go to the upper deck, she took his arm to lean on it heavily.

"Johnny, I won't give up. Please help me not to give up."

Johnny looked down at her with a reassuring smile.

As they stepped on deck they found themselves looking at a new world. Gone was the fog. In its place was racing blue waters, flecked with foam.

"A storm!" the girl shuddered.

"Just too dark to see land," Johnny groaned. "If it wasn't, we might get our location and then—"

"Then what?" she whispered.

"I have some plans. We—"

"Sh—an officer!" she warned.

At the evening meal Rusty ate hard, dry crackers and drank scalding tea. She was still putting up a brave struggle against being sea-sick.

When darkness came they went below. Rusty retired at once. Johnny threw himself, all dressed, upon his berth, but did not sleep.

An hour later a shadowy figure passed him. It was Rusty. She was carrying blankets. Without a sound, he followed her. Arrived on deck, he saw her at the rail. Understanding, he dropped down upon a wooden bench.

After what seemed a long time, she turned and saw him. Swaying as she walked, she came toward him to drop down at his side. She did not say, "I am so sick!" She was too game for that and there was no need. He wrapped her in the blankets. Then they sat there in silence.

The wind was rising steadily. It went whistling through the rigging. Ropes banged and yard-arms swayed. A shadow shot past them, a watch on duty. Lights shone on the blue-black sea. It was a truly wild night.

Of a sudden a form stood before them. Clutching a steel cable, it clung there.

"Thousand pardons," it hissed. "Cannot stay here. It is forbidden."

"My friend is sick. We stay." Johnny felt his anger rising.

"Thousand pardons," came once more. "Cannot stay."

"Million pardons," Johnny half rose. "We stay."

A hand reached out. It touched Rusty's shoulder. That was enough. Johnny leaped at the man. They went down in a heap. A second more and Johnny felt a steel clamp about his neck, or so it seemed.

"Jujitsu," he thought in sudden consternation. Throwing all his strength into an effort to break the man's grip, he failed. Coughing, trying to breathe, failing, strangling, he felt his strength going when, of a sudden, he caught the sound of a blow, then felt the hated arm relax. Ten seconds more and he was free.

"You—you hit him," he managed to breathe. "Is he dead?"

"No—no. Watch out!" the girl warned.

Just in time Johnny caught the man. This time, gripping him by collar and trousers, he dragged him from the floor. And then, screaming like some wild thing, the brown man found himself hanging out over an angry sea.

"Johnny, don't!" The girl's hand was on his arm.

"Oh, all—all right."

Swinging the brown man in, he dropped him on the deck. Like a scared rabbit, the intruder went racing off on all fours.

"Now I've done it," Johnny groaned as he dropped back in his place.

"Perhaps," said Rusty. "Still, you can't tell."

CHAPTER XXI
WALL OF GLASS

Rusty was not the only one disturbed by this storm. At the very moment when Johnny was at grips with the Oriental on the ship's deck, Lawrence, Blackie and George were battling for their very lives.

What had happened? The distance from the trapper's cabin to shore was, they had discovered, far greater than they had supposed. When at last the fog cleared they found themselves far from any shore on a black and threatening sea.

"Might as well keep headed for the mainland," was Blackie's decision.

Head for the mainland they did. After that, for hours, with the storm ever increasing in intensity, they rowed as never before.

The clumsy oars were rough and hard to manage. Lawrence's hands were soon blistered. Tearing strips from his shirt, he bound them up and rowed on.

Fortune favored them in one thing. They were going with the wind. Had they been forced to face into the storm, their boat would have been swamped at once. As it was, just as darkness began to fall the skiff began to fill.

"Lawrence, you start bailing," Blackie commanded. "George and I will row."

"Ya-as, sir, we'll row. Don't nebber doubt dat," George agreed. Then he began to sing,

"Roll, Jordan, roll.

Oh! Oh! Oh! I want to go dere

To hear old Jordan roll."

Lawrence thought with a shudder that he might be there to hear Jordan roll before day dawned.

By constant bailing he was able to keep the skiff from swamping. So, chilled to the bone, hoping against hope, he labored on.

When at last they found themselves near to some shore, his heart failed him.

"Towering rocks," he groaned.

"There's a break in those rocks," said Blackie. "I saw it before dark. We'll follow along and here's hoping." Once more he put his stout shoulders to the oars.

A half hour passed, an hour, two hours. Numb with cold and ready to drop from exhaustion, Lawrence wondered if Blackie could have been wrong. Was there a break in that wall? And then—he saw it.

"There!" he exclaimed. "There it is. Straight ahead!"

He dared not add that it seemed a strange break. Not very deep, it appeared to give off an odd sort of glimmer at its back.

Just as they were ready to enter the gap, a great cloud went over the moon and all was black.

Steering more from instinct than sight, they rowed on. To Lawrence, at that moment, the suspense was all but overpowering. Where were they going? Could they find a landing? What was the end to be?

One thing was encouraging, the waves in this place were not so wild. They no longer dashed into the boat. So with darkness hanging over them they rowed, for what seemed an endless time, but could have been only a few moments, straight on into the unknown.

And then. "Man! Oh, man! What was that?" The boat had crashed into an invisible wall.

Lawrence put out a hand. "Glass!" he exclaimed. "A wall of glass."

"Not glass, son," Blackie's voice was low. "A wall of ice. The end of a glacier. This is a spot where icebergs break off. If one of them had been jarred loose by the bang of our boat—and if they had been sent tumbling by the sound of a voice—man! Oh, man! We would be lost for good and all."

"Blackie, look!" Lawrence spoke in a hoarse whisper. "A light."

"It's a star," said Blackie.

"A light," Lawrence insisted.

"Yas, man! A light," George agreed.

Just then the moon came out, revealing a sloping mountain side. And, close to a shelving beach was a cabin. The light shone from that cabin.

"Oh! Oh! Lord be praised!" George whispered fervently.

Ten minutes later, as they drew their boat up on the beach, the cabin door was thrown open and a man, holding a candle close to his face, peered into the darkness to call, "You all come right on up, whoever you all are."

"That," said Lawrence in a surprised whisper, "is Smokey Joe."

"Smokey Joe, you old bear-cat!" Blackie shouted.

The grizzled prospector let out a dry cackle. "Come on up an' rest yerself," he welcomed. "I got a Mulligan on a-cookin'."

At first Lawrence found it hard to believe that this was really Smokey Joe. "How," he asked himself, "could he come all this way?" As he studied a faded map on the deserted cabin's wall, however, he realized that the distance overland was short compared to the way they had traveled by water.

Joe's Mulligan stew proved a rich repast. He had killed a young caribou two days before. There had been bacon and hardtack in his kit. Besides these, he had found dried beans and seasoning in the cabin.

"Yep," he agreed, as Blackie complimented him after the meal was over, "hit's plum grand livin' when you sort of git the breaks.

"An' listen," his voice dropped. "Hit's plumb quare how things git to a comin' yer way. Yesterday I found gold. Struck hit rich, you might say." From a moose-hide sack he tumbled a handful of nuggets.

"Gold!" Blackie exclaimed.

"Yup. Hit's might nigh pure gold," the old man agreed. "Nuther thing that's plumb quare. Hit's nigh onto that little blue bear's den."

"What?" Lawrence started up. "A blue bear! A—a glacier bear?"

"Reckon you might call 'em that," the old man agreed.

"He's been a-stayin' in a sort of cave up thar fer a right smart spell."

"How—how far is it?" Lawrence asked almost in a whisper.

"Hit—I reckon hit's—" the old man studied for a moment. "Why, hit's right about three peaks, a look an' a right smart."

"What does that mean?" Blackie asked in a surprised tone.

"Wall, you jest climb one of them thar least mounting peaks," the old man explained. "Then another, an' another."

"Three peaks," said Blackie.

"Fer startin'," said Smokey Joe. "Arter that you take a look an' hit's a right smart furder than you can see."

"Perhaps about ten miles," suggested Blackie after they had had a good laugh, which Smokey Joe took good-naturedly.

"Near on to that," the old man agreed.

Long after the old man had rolled himself in his blankets and fallen asleep Lawrence and Blackie sat beside the cracked stove talking.

"Blackie," Lawrence said in a husky voice, "that little blue bear is worth a lot of money. The Professor told us he'd trade us a tractor for one. They're rare, about the rarest animals on earth. There's not one in captivity anywhere."

"That won't help much," Blackie grumbled. "If this wind goes down, we've got to get out of here at dawn. Something's happened to Johnny and MacGregor. We've got to look for them."

"Yes," Lawrence agreed. "But if the wind doesn't go down?"

"We'll have to stay here," said Blackie. "And," with a low chuckle, "we might go 'three peaks, a look and a right smart' looking for your blue-eyed bear."

CHAPTER XXII
DREAMS

"Johnny," Rusty's voice was low, husky with strangely mingled emotions, "when we are back at the cottage, I'll make a big pan of ice-box cookies. We'll take them with a big bottle of hot cocoa. We'll go out on a sunny rock and have a feast." They were still on the deck of the rolling ship and it was still night.

Rusty's voice rose. "And such sunshine! Nowhere in the world is it so glorious."

"All right," Johnny agreed. "Ice-box cookies, hot chocolate and sunshine. That will be keen."

"Dreams," he was thinking. "How often when things are hard, very hard, we dream." As he closed his eyes now he could see dead salmon in endless rows. He could hear the monotonous drone of brown men and the endless wash-wash of the sea. "How grand at times to dream of other things far away!" he said. "And what a joy to know of other places where we have been gloriously happy."

"Yes," she agreed, "that is wonderful. And Johnny," she went on, "we have a home in Seattle, father and I. It is small, but, oh, so beautiful! Climbing roses and pine trees. There's a lake before it. There is a dancing pavilion not far away where the boys and girls I know best come. There they swing and sway to bewitching waltz time. *Over the Waves, Blue Danube* and all the rest. Johnny, will you come sometime and join us there?" Her voice seemed dreamy and far away.

"Yes," said Johnny. "Some day I'll come."

"But first," he thought savagely, "I'll see this infernal boat at the bottom of the sea."

For a time after that they were silent. Once again they heard the beating of ropes against spars, the wail of the wind and the dash of spray on the deck. How was all this to end?

"Rusty," Johnny said, "I would like to leave you for a while."

"Why?"

"There's something I want to do. You know," he leaned close, speaking in a hoarse whisper, "there's a hole in the gas tank of your boat."

"Yes, but—"

"We may get a break. Your boat was put on deck after two others. That means they'll have to put her in the water before taking the others off. If there was gas in her tank we might slip down to her and get away."

"But the gas, Johnny?"

"There are two large cans in another boat. I saw them. I—I'm going to plug up that hole in your tank, then try to fill it from the cans."

"They—they may catch you." Her voice trembled.

"I'll take a chance." He rose without a sound. "I'm off. If I don't come back, tell good old MacGregor."

"I—I'll tell him." Her whisper was lost in the wind. He was gone.

Creeping along the swaying deck, dodging behind a lifeboat when the watch appeared, scooting forward, then pausing to listen, he at last reached the side of the *Krazy Kat*.

After securing the cans of gasoline, he lifted them to the deck of Rusty's small boat. Then, with a deft swing, he threw himself after the cans. The deck was wet with fog. Slipping, he went down in a heap, but made no sound.

Feeling about in the dark, he found the tank and the leak. A sharpened splinter of wood stopped the hole.

"Now the gas," he whispered. This he knew would be most dangerous of all. Cans have a way of gurgling and popping in an alarming manner. The gurgle, he concluded, would not matter. It would not be heard above the roar of the wind and the wash of the sea. But the tinny bangs? Ah, well, he'd have to risk it.

When one can was emptied into the *Krazy Kat's* tank, he heaved a sigh of relief. The second was half-emptied when he caught the sound of footsteps.

"The watch!" Consternation seized him. Flattening himself on the deck, he clung to the still gurgling can.

The sound of footsteps ceased. His heart pounded. Was he caught? Seconds seemed minutes. If the can popped he was lost. Ten seconds, twenty, thirty—again the footsteps. Then they grew indistinct in the distance.

"Ah," the boy breathed.

Just then the all but empty can gave forth a loud bang!

Johnny jumped, then lay flat, listening with all his ears. For at least two full minutes he remained there motionless. The watch did not return.

With great care he lifted the empty cans from the deck of the *Krazy Kat* to toss them into the foaming sea. Then, stealthily as before, he made his way back to Rusty's side.

"I—I did it," he shrilled. "Now for a good break and we're away."

"Here—here's hoping." She drew her hand from beneath the blankets to grip his own.

"MacGregor, what do you think they'll do to me?" Johnny asked an hour later. The storm had partially subsided. Rusty was feeling better. They were back in their staterooms. Johnny had told the old man of the night's adventure.

"It's my opinion," said MacGregor, "that you'll be shot at sunrise."

"That won't be so bad," said Johnny, joining in the joke.

"Not half-bad," MacGregor agreed. "I mind an Eskimo we shot up there in the far north. He'd killed a white man. The revenue cutter came along an' the judge tried him.

"When the judge's decision had been arrived at, they told this Eskimo to stand up.

"Well, sir, he stood there stiff an' straight as any soldier. He was sure he had been condemned to die and that he was to be shot. They're a sturdy lot, those Eskimos.

"Well," MacGregor paused to laugh. "They set a thing up an' aimed it at the Eskimo. Something clicked. The Eskimo blinked. But nothin' else happened.

"The white men folded things up and left. But the Eskimo still stood there, not knowin', I suppose, whether he was dead or alive.

"Know what happened?" he concluded. "He'd been found innocent and they had taken his picture.

"For all I know," he added, "he's livin' still an' so'll you be, me boy, forty years from today.

"What can they do?" he demanded. "They don't dare harm us."

"I wouldn't trust them too far," said Johnny.

"Nor I," Rusty agreed.

CHAPTER XXIII
IN THE BLUE BEAR'S CAVE

It was with a feeling of great uneasiness that Johnny came on deck next morning. What was to happen? Had that little brown man told the story of their struggle in the night? And if he had? He shuddered.

Yet, strange to say, the day wore on in perfect peace. They were not even asked to go below and clean fish. The reason for this was apparent, the fish on deck had been taken care of. Since the storm was still roaring across the sea, no others could be brought in. During the forenoon two small, motor-driven crafts came close to stand by.

"They belong to this outfit," MacGregor declared. "They may have salmon below-deck. They're afraid of the storm. That's why they don't come in."

"Ah, well," he sighed. "We're here for the day at least. Even if your *Krazy Kat* was in the water, Rusty, we couldn't risk her in a storm like this."

"These Orientals are a queer lot," Johnny mused.

"Queer's no name for it, me boy," said MacGregor. "As for me, I don't trust 'em. They're like children, just when they're makin' the least noise is when you're sure they're up to some mischief."

Was this true? Johnny shuddered anew, but said never a word.

They discovered during their lunch in their stateroom at noon that there was something vaguely familiar about the brown boy who brought the lunch. Johnny stared at him. But Rusty exclaimed in a whisper, "Kopkina! You here?"

The boy made a motion for silence. "I am spy," he whispered. "Red McGee good man. Me, I, Red McGee man.

"You listen," his voice dropped to a whisper. "I tell 'em, that one captain this ship, tell 'em you Red McGee boy." He nodded to Rusty. "Tell 'em Red McGee mebby plenty mad. Plenty 'fraid Red McGee. They not punish you for fight on deck last night. Must go now." He disappeared through the door.

"Boy!" Johnny breathed. "I'm feeling better already."

Two hours later they had added cause for feeling better. Just when the sea was beginning to calm a little they caught the drum of a motor. As Johnny heard it his heart stood still, then leaped.

"A motor," he breathed. "That's a powerful motor. If only it's Dan MacMillan and his seaplane."

"It is! It is!" Rusty's voice rose to a high pitch. "There! There it is. See!"

Johnny did see. He pointed it out to MacGregor. They all leaned on the rail watching the seaplane approach.

"If it's only Dan," MacGregor breathed.

There came the sound of rushing feet. Apparently every little brown man on the boat had heard those motors. They came swarming onto the deck.

"If it's Dan MacMillan," said MacGregor, "there's sure to be someone with him."

"They'll be looking for us," said Rusty.

"Yes, and we'll have to find a way to let them know we're here," Johnny added.

"That," said MacGregor, "is going to be hard, with all these." His glance swept the brown throng.

"Tell you what!" Johnny exclaimed. "Rusty and I might do a little boxing bout. There's sure to be someone on the plane who knows us."

"And they'll recognize you by your actions," MacGregor agreed. "It's a capital idea. I'll go for the gloves."

And so it happened that, as the seaplane flew over the ship, circled, then dipping low, passed within a hundred feet, those in it witnessed a strange sight—two white youngsters staging a boxing match for the benefit of a host of little brown men, who, truth to tell, gave them scant attention.

"I only hope they recognized us," said Johnny, throwing his gloves on the deck.

"You and me too," said Rusty. "Anyway," she laughed, "that's one time I didn't knock you out."

Whatever impression this little drama may have made upon the occupants of the seaplane, the effect of the appearance of the seaplane on the little brown men was apparent at once. On every face as the seaplane went winging away MacGregor read consternation.

"They're afraid," he grumbled low to his young companions. "Down deep in their hearts they are afraid."

"What will they do now?" Rusty asked anxiously.

"They're already doin' it," said MacGregor, calling attention to the rush and bustle on board. "Puttin' the ship in shape. It wouldn't surprise me if they weighed anchor within the hour. And if they do, me lassie," he added, "you may be lookin' on them Oriental cities within a week, for they'll be headin' straight for home."

"Oh-o," Rusty breathed. But she said never a word.

On that same morning in Smokey Joe's cabin Lawrence was up before the wee small hours had passed. After one good look at the sea, which was still rolling high, he dashed back into the cabin to find Blackie staring at him wide awake.

"Black-Blackie," he stammered. "I—I hate to disturb you. But—but that blue bear—"

"I know." Blackie sat up. "Three peaks, a look and a right smart ho, hum."

"Blackie! It's terribly important. Just think! A little blue bear. The only one in captivity, if we get him."

"I know." Blackie slid out of his bunk. "Get the fire going. Put the coffee pot on. We'll be off in a half hour."

"Oh, think—"

"Put the coffee on!" Blackie roared.

After tacking an old shirt to a pole as a signal of distress to any boat that might pass and instructing Smokey Joe to be on the lookout, Blackie drew a rough map, showing where, according to Smokey's direction, the bear's cave might be found. After that he led the way over the first "peak."

These peaks were, they discovered, mere ridges. The distance was, in reality, much shorter than they had thought.

"This is the place," Lawrence said, an hour and a half later. "It must be."

"It is," Blackie agreed. "There are the two scrub spruce trees with Smokey's blaze on them."

"And there's the cave!" Lawrence was greatly excited.

"Not much of a cave," said Blackie. "Might be quite some bear at that. Wait."

With a small hatchet he hacked away at a dry spruce knot until he had a pitch-filled torch. This, with the aid of some dry shavings, he lighted.

"Now," he breathed. "Give me one of the ropes. We'll have to manage to tangle him up somehow. I'll lead the way."

"Al-all right," Lawrence's tongue was dry.

The floor of the dark grotto was strewn with pebbles. To walk without making a noise was impossible.

"Wait! Listen!" Lawrence whispered when they had covered some twenty paces.

As they paused, they caught a low hissing sound.

"Snakes," the boy suggested.

"Not here. Too cold. It's the bear. Get your rope ready."

Slowly, cautiously they moved forward.

"There! There are his eyes." Two balls of fire appeared directly before them.

And then things began to happen. A low snarl was followed by the sound of scattered pebbles. Blackie was hit by the rushing bear and bowled over like a ten pin. But Lawrence, quick as a cat, saw a hairy head, aimed a short swing and let go his rope.

Next instant he was shouting: "Blackie! Quick! Help! I got him! I got him!"

The husky little blue bear dragged them both to the very entrance of the cave. There, panting and tearing at the rope, he paused to glare at them. The rope was drawn tight about his shoulders with one foreleg through the loop.

Blackie, who was both fast and strong, made quick work of what remained to be done. Fifteen minutes later, carrying the live bear slung between them on a pole, they headed for the cabin.

To their great joy, as they neared the cabin, they saw one of Red McGee's gill-net boats awaiting them in the little bay. Smokey Joe had flagged it down.

After a hasty, "Thank you and goodbye" to Smokey, they tossed their priceless captive into the after cabin of the stout, little motor-boat to head straight away over a rolling sea toward still more adventure, of quite a different nature.

CHAPTER XXIV
OVERTAKING A SHADOW

Once again it was night. The wind had gone down with the sun. The sea was calm. On board the Oriental ship there was a strained air of tense expectancy.

"I can't understand what's keepin' 'em here," MacGregor said in a low tone to his young companions. "It's plain that they're scared stiff of that seaplane. Looks like they'd heave anchor and be away any minute. And if they do—" There was no need to finish. Both Johnny and Rusty knew that this would mean a trip to the Orient under circumstances stranger than any fiction.

"They seem to be waiting for something," said Johnny.

This was true. All the little brown men not stationed at posts of duty were standing along the rail looking away toward the distant shores that were lost in the night.

"They'll be back," MacGregor said, thinking of the men on the seaplane. "Looks like it's a race against time. But what are they waiting for?"

It was not long until they should know. As they stood there, nerves a-tingle, listening, a distant confusion of noises came to them.

"If there were a war," said MacGregor, "I'd say it was rifle and machine-gun fire."

This notion was too fantastic to be seriously considered. But what was it?

Second by second the sound increased in volume. "Can this be what they're looking for?" Johnny asked.

If so, these little men welcomed it in a strange manner. Short, sharp commands were given. Scores of men went into frenzied action.

"Look!" Rusty gripped Johnny's arm. "They're lowering my boat into the water."

"And it's got gas in the tank. All ready to turn over and start. If only—"

"That's motors we're hearin'," MacGregor broke in. "A thunderin' lot of 'em! I shouldn't wonder—"

"MacGregor," Rusty seized his arm, "our boat is in the water. They are all crowding the rail again. This may be our chance."

"So it may," the old man agreed. "Follow me. Not a sound!"

"I'll get Kopkina," offered Johnny. "I just saw him on deck."

Dodging behind a life-raft Rusty and MacGregor went scurrying along in the dark and Johnny and Kopkina soon joined them.

"It—it's just here," Rusty whispered.

"We—we need a rope ladder," Johnny exclaimed low.

"Here's one," came in MacGregor's cheering voice. "Let her over easy now."

"Now," he breathed. "Over you go."

The speed with which they went down that ladder, all but treading on one another's fingers, would have done credit to the U. S. Navy.

"Now I'll cut her loose," said MacGregor. "All right, Rusty, turn her over."

The fly-wheel whirled. The splendid motor began a low put-put-put. They were away into the dark.

"They'd have trouble findin' us," MacGregor murmured.

"But listen!" Johnny exclaimed.

The sound of many motors had doubled and redoubled. Just as they were about to swing around the prow of the ship, something long, dark and silent shot past them.

"The Shadow!" Johnny exclaimed.

It was true, this was the Shadow. But at last the Shadow was not going to escape. After it thundered a powerful speedboat and as she shot past them the excited trio saw a burst of flames and caught the rat-tat-tat of a machine gun.

This was followed instantly by a wild scream from the Shadow which sounded very much like a sign of surrender. At the same time the sea seemed fairly ablaze with lights from many boats.

Johnny's head was in a whirl. What was happening? Without knowing why she did it, Rusty seized him by the arm and held him tight while she screamed, "Johnny! It's wonderful! Wonderful!"

What had happened may be quickly told. When Blackie and his crew failed to return, and Rusty as well, there had been consternation about the cannery. There was little use searching Bristol Bay in a fog. When, however, Dan MacMillan appeared in his seaplane, they went into action. Red McGee climbed into the cockpit and they were away. They had circled for an hour when they sighted the Oriental ship.

As they flew over it Red McGee experienced no difficulty in getting the unusual signals Johnny and Rusty had set up for him. He recognized the boxing forms of both Rusty and Johnny.

Realizing that his daughter would be on board that ship only against her will, he went into a wild rage. He demanded that the seaplane be landed close to the ship and that he be allowed to "tackle the whole lot of 'em single-handed."

To this young MacMillan, would not consent; for, in the first place, the sea was too rough for a landing and in the second, he was not willing as he later expressed it, "To see a good man commit suicide by tackling a hundred Orientals single-handed."

He had flown back to their base. By the time they reached the cannery, Red had cooled off.

"I want every last boat gassed up for an emergency run," he commanded. "Any of you men that have guns, get 'em loaded and ready. There's a couple o' whale-guns up at my cabin. You, Pete and Dan, get 'em an' see that they're loaded. We'll show 'em."

They were about ready for a start when Blackie and his men arrived on the scene.

"Blackie," Red exploded, "they've got Rusty and your boy, Johnny. They're holdin' 'em captive. Come on! We'll start a war!"

For once, Blackie did not say, "No." After they had turned the small, blue bear loose in a sheet-metal tool-shed he climbed into Dan MacMillan's speed boat, dragging Red and Lawrence with him, and they were away.

It was this speedboat that had spied the Shadow. They had given it chase and had, as you have seen, at last, after sending a volley of machine-gun bullets across its bow, overhauled it.

The Shadow was the very craft that had been awaited by the Oriental ship. Had it put in an appearance two hours sooner, the ship must surely have weighed anchor and our story might have been much longer. As it was, the Orientals were destined to wait a long, long time before lifting the Shadow on deck, if at all.

While Johnny and Rusty looked and listened, the whole cannery fleet, every small deck bristling with guns, surrounded the ship.

Having overhauled the Shadow, Blackie placed it in charge of another craft, then came gliding in alongside the *Krazy Kat*.

"MacGregor," he said in a husky voice, "tell me what happened." MacGregor told him. Hardly had he finished when a small motor launch carrying three little brown officers arrived. The officers were fairly aglow with gold and braid.

"A thousand pardons," their leader began. He was allowed to go no farther.

"Listen!" Blackie stood up. He was dressed in corduroy trousers and a leather jacket. His face was working strangely.

"Listen," he repeated. "No apologies, not a thousand, nor even one. I'll do the talking." His voice was low. "I know why you're here. To catch our fish. You sank our boat. You have an hour to get your ship headed out of Bristol Bay. We'll take that Shadow of yours with us. We caught her lifting nets inside the three-mile limit. That makes her a fair prize.

"As to the sinking of the *Stormy Petrel*, I shall make a complete report. The matter shall be taken up by our diplomats.

"I might add, for your further information, that a law is now before our Congress making Bristol Bay United States waters, open to our fishermen alone. It will pass. If you care to come back next year we will meet you with three destroyers.

"And now, gentlemen," he doffed a ragged cap, "I bid you good-night."

Clicking their heels, without a single apology, the officers saluted, then the power boat lost itself in the shadows.

CHAPTER XXV
"BILL" RETURNS

"Rusty, my child," said Red McGee, springing aboard the *Krazy Kat* as soon as the Orientals were gone, "are you all right?"

"Never better," Rusty laughed. "And never half so excited. I—I'm all right," she added, "except that I'll have to grow a new crop of curls."

"Curls," Red chuckled. "They're not very necessary. Not even for a girl."

"Going back with us in the speed boat?" he asked.

"No-o, if you don't mind," she hesitated. "We've been together so long, the three of us, MacGregor, Johnny, and I, that I—I think we'd like to follow you back in the *Krazy Kat.*"

"O.K.," Red agreed. "Kopkina, suppose you come with me. I want to thank you for what you've done for us. Now let's get going."

Already the Oriental ship that had never been welcome was slipping out into the night.

On the way back Johnny and Rusty spent most of their time studying the stars and the moon. Just what they read there only they will ever know.

The secret of the Shadow was found to be quite simple, as most secrets are. It was a long, low craft without deck, cabins, rails or riggings. Powered by large storage batteries, it was able to slip in close to shore, set a three-mile-long net at night and lift it in the morning. The fish were rushed to other motor-boats outside the three-mile zone and were then carried to the floating cannery.

After installing a gasoline motor, Blackie used the Shadow for sea patrol. No demand for the return of the craft was made. Needless to say, the duties of Blackie, MacGregor, Johnny and Lawrence were exceedingly light for the remainder of the season.

The small blue bear throve on fish-cleanings and other scraps. He was fat and friendly when at last the boys headed for Seward and Matanuska Valley. At Seward they left him in the care of a friend until they could come in a small truck and cart him home.

At the cabin in the valley Johnny and Lawrence were given an uproarious welcome.

One thing surprised them—the Professor was back. "I am waiting for Bill," he explained.

"Bill! Who's he?" Lawrence asked. "Oh!" he exclaimed. "He's the man who built the shelter and left a note saying he was coming back. Let me see—"

"Today," said the Professor. "And here he is now." A smiling young giant with a full red beard came tramping down the road.

"Bill, did you get one?" the Professor demanded.

"No," Bill's smile faded. "I did my best. I got the head and hide of one, that's all. Had to kill him, or lose him. I—I'm sorry."

"A whole year," the Professor groaned. "And never a bear."

"A bear!" Johnny exclaimed. "Surely there are bears a-plenty."

"Not that kind," the Professor corrected. "I want the kind we talked about once, a glacier bear. Nothing else counts."

"Oh, a glacier bear!" Lawrence laughed happily. "Is that all you want? I have one coming up on a truck from Seward. It should be here any time."

"Just like that!" Bill dropped weakly down upon a stump. "A whole year. Ice, snow, blizzards, glaciers, hunger, a whole year. Never a bear. And now this boy calmly says, 'I've got one coming up.'"

"Such," said the professor, "is the luck of the chase."

There was time for Bill to satisfy his craving for a "real feed." Then the truck arrived.

The Professor and Bill gave one look at the little blue glacier bear. Then, for sheer joy, they fell into each other's arms.

"What do you want for him?" the Professor demanded at last.

"A tractor," said Lawrence.

"The best in the settlement!"

"The Titan."

"Agreed and for good measure, a gang plow, a harrow, two drums of gas and three log chains."

Lawrence could not say a word. He could only stand and stare. All his dreams had come true in a moment.

"I only wish we might do better," the Professor half apologized. "But we've spent a great deal of money in the search. So-o, I—"

"I think," said Lawrence, "that you're a very good sport. And—and we thank you."

Three days later Johnny and Lawrence were in Seward for a day with Blackie when a trim power boat glided up to the dock.

"Hello, Johnny!" came in a girl's voice. It was Rusty.

"Come on down to Seattle with us," Red McGee boomed.

"We'll show you a roarin' good time, just to celebrate the finest salmon season ever known."

"What do you say?" Johnny turned to Lawrence.

"You go," said Lawrence. "I'm a farmer now. I've got to stay with my crops, and I'm anxious to get started with the new tractor."

Johnny went. If there were further adventures awaiting him at the end of that short journey you may find them recorded in a book called, *Sign of the Green Arrow.*

Booksophile
Your Local Online Bookstore

Buy Books Online from
www.Booksophile.com

Explore our collection of books written in various languages and uncommon topics from different parts of the world, including history, art and culture, poems, autobiography and bibliographies, cooking, action & adventure, world war, fiction, science, and law.

Add to your bookshelf or gift to another lover of books - first editions of some of the most celebrated books ever published. From classic literature to bestsellers, you will find many first editions that were presumed to be out-of-print.

Free shipping globally for orders worth US$ 100.00.

Use code "Shop_10" to avail additional 10% on first order.

Visit today
www.booksophile.com

Milton Keynes UK
Ingram Content Group UK Ltd.
UKHW011834071223
433887UK00004B/485

9 789357 972802